V35t

A TIME OF
TROUBLES

A TIME OF TROUBLES

PIETER VAN RAVEN

CHARLES SCRIBNER'S SONS • NEW YORK

Collier Macmillan Canada • Toronto
Maxwell Macmillan International Publishing Group
New York • Oxford • Singapore • Sydney

This novel is a work of fiction. Any references to historical events, to real people living or dead, or to real locales are intended only to give the work a setting in historical reality. Other names, characters, places, and incidents are the product of the author's imagination.

Charles Scribner's Sons Books for Young Readers
Macmillan Publishing Company
866 Third Avenue, New York, NY 10022
Collier Macmillan Canada, Inc.
1200 Eglinton Avenue East, Suite 200
Don Mills, Ontario M3C 3N1

Printed in the United States of America
First Edition   10 9 8 7 6 5 4 3 2 1

Library of Congress Cataloging-in-Publication Data
van Raven, Pieter, 1923–
A time of troubles/Pieter van Raven.—1st ed.   p.   cm.
Summary: Having crossed the country with his father during the depression to find work in California, fourteen-year-old Roy encounters cruel exploitation by the Growers' Association of the desperate, impoverished people pouring into the state.
[1. Depression—1929—Fiction. 2. Migrant labor—Fiction.] I. Title.
PZ7.V347Ti 1990   [Fic]—dc20   90-31409   CIP   AC
ISBN 0-684-19212-8

For Paula

A TIME OF TROUBLES

1

From the bus station to the prison took about an hour's walk. By now Roy knew every rusty Neehi and Burma Shave sign and every broken fence post along the way by heart. Dust blew up from the road. Twice in the last four years, he recollected, they had tarred the narrow little road, but the dirt underneath kept pressing up through the tar and after a while you couldn't even tell it was supposed to be a paved road.

Once, a couple of years back, Roy had seen the tar truck. It went down the road ahead of him, a black truck with a long pipe in back with holes in it. A man leaned against the truck. Every once in a while he turned a gummy wheel and cut off the shower of tar. When the truck stopped, he got off and ran a piece of wire into some of the holes in the pipe that were clogged up. Then he turned the wheel and shouted to the driver. The tank truck lurched on toward the prison. That was the end of the road. The truck was coming back before Roy got to the prison.

For a while after that, until the frost came and

the tar got hard, you had to walk on the sandy path beside the road. On Sundays there was a steady line of folks, black and white both, passing down the path from the bus depot in Milford to the prison to visit their relatives and friends and sweethearts. Some of the young women, in high heels and silk stockings to make themselves pretty for their boyfriends, teetered so in the sand, they had to roll down their stockings and take off their shoes and stockings until they got to the prison wall, where they bent over and put them back on.

Cars, too, came along to the prison. Model A's and a few Model T's or a farm truck that sometimes might stop to pick you up if you stuck out your thumb. Mostly it was a black folks' truck that pulled over to the side and waited while you swung your bottom up over the tailgate. The white drivers kept on going down the sticky road, their eyes fixed straight ahead so it would seem they hadn't noticed you. Once in a great while a Buick or Packard would roll by, the driver in a coat and tie and hat. The big cars never stopped.

They were lawyers, Roy knew, lawyers who were coming to talk to a prisoner about getting him out or bringing him something to sign, or, Dad said, cooking up some deal. None of them was coming to see Dad, that was for sure, Roy told himself. The only person coming to visit him was his son Roy.

The first Sunday of every month—Roy had them marked on the feed store calendar—he walked to the depot in Tilson with his paper bag of things for Dad: some westerns with the covers ripped off the drugstore couldn't sell and let him have two for a nickel, a package of chocolate cupcakes Dad was partial to, four freshly washed and ironed blue denim shirts to get him through the month, and a sandwich for Roy to eat along the way.

After the first time, Mom never went back to the prison. That day she took Roy up to the desk. "This is Roy Purdy, Harlow Purdy's boy. He'll be coming to visit his dad once a month. I'd be obliged if you'd let him in. I got a baby at home to look after, and I can't come on my own." They made Mom sign a paper, and that took care of that.

Four to six years, the judge had said when Dad pleaded guilty to setting fire to Cochran's packing plant with malicious intent. For over four years now, Roy had been getting off the bus at Milford with his paper bag and walking down the tar road to the prison. Sometimes with an old man who got off the bus, too, although he hadn't got on in Tilson with Roy. He didn't know the old man's name. Roy walked slowly to let the old man keep up. They didn't talk much, but the old man always explained that he was going to see his son. "One hundred and ninety-nine years they gave him," he repeated. "They might as well have given him the rope. That's more than two lifetimes, ain't it, boy? Sam said he was sorry he shot that woman in the bank. I reckon he is now. He didn't even get the money. When the gun went off he ran right out the doors of the bank straight into a policeman. Don't that beat all?"

Roy hadn't seen the old man the last couple of months. He wondered if something had happened to him. Inside, he used to see him farther down the bench leaning forward to the heavy wire mesh talking to a large bald-headed man. Dad said Sam stayed pretty much to himself, the way most of the lifers did.

George the guard waved him on through to the steel door. "Got your bag, do you, Roy? I don't reckon I'll have to look at it. Your pa won't be figuring on busting out today." Seeing the boy's surprise he said, "You didn't know? Harlow's got himself released."

2

Ruth Ann listened calmly. "He was bound to get out sooner or later. It looks like he got out sooner, don't it? Take your finger out of your mouth, Lilian. You're too big to be sucking on your fingers. When are they turning him loose, Roy? Did they say?"

"Dad said next week, on Thursday."

"Well, I have my plans made." Ruth Ann pulled open the drawer of the kitchen table. Deep in back of the silver section and the knives and the can opener was where she kept her money. She snapped the rubber band off a roll of dirty dollar bills. She smoothed them out on the table. Slowly she counted them, ". . . thirty-one, thirty-two, thirty-three. Seems like there was more than that here. You didn't take none, did you, Roy?"

Roy shook his head. He kept his wages from the boat shed in the old wallet Dad had left with him. He knew to the penny how much he had: seventeen dollars in bills and thirty-five cents in the coin pocket. He gave Mom most of what he earned to run the house.

"I remember now. I gave the doctor five dollars for

Lilian's chicken pox. Five dollars just for looking down her throat and a jar of salve to put on her itch. I used it all up the first night. No matter, I got enough money to get us there."

"Where, Mom, where you going? Dad's coming home. We'll be all right now."

"I only stayed here because you're Harlow's boy. I didn't have the heart to carry you off while he was in prison. He's coming out now, and I'm moving back home where he can't get at me."

"But . . ." the boy protested.

"Roy, when they open the gates to let Harlow out, he's going to do two things straightaway. First, he's going to get drunk if he has any money. The second thing he's going to do is beat me up. Not like he used to, but worse, a whole lot worse."

"He's changed, Mom. He won't do that. He's sorry for what he done, he keeps telling me. 'Just wait till I get out,' he keeps saying. 'Tell Ruth Ann I'll make it up to her. She won't have to crack crabs anymore at the fishhouse.'"

"Who do you think's going to give Harlow a job after he burnt down the packing plant? He put a couple of dozen people out of work. These are hard times, Roy. They ain't going to forget what he done. And it won't take him long to find out I told the sheriff how he came home drunk the day they fired him and went off down the road when it got dark with a can of coal oil. I didn't tell the sheriff on purpose—he sort of eased it out of me before I caught on—but that won't make no nevermind to Harlow."

"You going all the way back to West Virginia?" Roy asked sadly.

6

"I am. With Lilian, and you, too, if you are of a mind to go. President Roosevelt's got the mines working again. Daddy was the first man in Webster Springs to go back down. Ma can look after Lilian, and I'll find me something to do in town. Good times are coming, Ma said. Daddy's talking about getting an automobile. How about that Roy, a real automobile? You want to come along? You can go back to school."

"I can't do that," Roy replied. "Dad's going to need someone looking after him. He's no good in the house. And maybe, like you say, he won't be getting a job right off." What Roy didn't say was that he didn't want to spend the rest of his growing-up in a West Virginia coal mining town. They promised at the boat shed that next year they'd take him on regular at fifty cents an hour. That was four dollars a day, more than Mom made when she could find someone to look after Lilian so she could go to the fishhouse.

"Well, you think on it, Roy, and let me know. You ain't my boy, so I got no claim to make you come with me. But Lilian, she's mine, you tell Dad, and she stays with me. Lilian wouldn't even know who Harlow was if he walked through the door this very minute."

When Roy came home from the boat shed Monday evening, Mom and Lilian were gone. He reckoned they took the bus down to Cape Charles and the ferry over to Norfolk. He picked up the note from the table.

Tell yor dad I'm sorry. I done rite by his boy wile he was away. if you chanje yr mind daddy can find a plase for you in the mines. lilian say's goodby.

Mom.

Roy walked around the four rooms, the heavy sound of his boots echoing through the shack. Mom hadn't even taken all her clothes. She must have been late for the bus. Her old felt slippers were under the bed, along with the rag doll Dad had made for Lilian in the prison. He hadn't managed to sew the two black buttons for eyes on straight, according to Lilian, and she didn't pay much attention to Mary Jane, the name Dad had stitched across the front of the doll's overalls.

Roy picked up Mary Jane. He'd have to hide her somewhere. There was no point in making Dad unhappy right after he got out. Maybe Mom and Lilian would be coming back if he wrote later on that Dad had a regular job and given up drinking.

Everything else Mom had left in place. Roy filled the bucket from the pump by the back steps. He washed the creosote off his arms with the yellow laundry soap. In the icebox Mom had left some cold potatoes and part of a boiled chicken. The ice was almost melted. Roy reached up to turn around the yellow card in the window, so the truck would stop to leave a block of ice in the box. Mom hadn't left any change in the kitchen drawer. Roy counted twenty-five cents from his wallet and left it on the corner of the table for the ice man. They'd have to go easy with his savings, Roy told himself, until Dad got a regular job.

3

Roy remembered what Mom had said about Dad getting drunk the minute they let him out of prison. He didn't believe Dad would, but he did recall there were some bottles of beer and a couple of cans of Silver Dime in the cooler at the bus depot in Milford where Roy spent a precious dime on a Dr Pepper one hot afternoon when the bus was late.

He had better not take any chances. On Wednesday he asked Mr. Whitlock if he could take the next day off because his father was coming home and he'd better go over to the prison in case Dad didn't have any money to get home.

Mr. Whitlock looked at him real hard. "They pay those men in prison for what they do. I hear it isn't much, but they pay them. Didn't Harlow tell you that?"

Roy shook his head.

"Harlow must have made upwards of a hundred dollars in four years, wouldn't you say, Maynard?" Mr. Whitlock asked his boat builder, who Roy was going to help regular next year.

9

"Unless he drank it up," Maynard said. "The guards slip the men things they oughtn't to have."

"I think Dad stopped drinking," Roy said defensively. "He wasn't a real drunk, anyway."

"No, I reckon he wasn't," Maynard replied. "He just liked to drink all the time. And he just happened by accident to be drunk when he set the packing plant on fire and burnt it to the ground."

"If he did it, it was because they fired him for no cause," Roy argued.

"So Harlow went back and fired twenty or more people that night," Maynard said sarcastically, "including my daughter. She ain't had a proper job since."

Roy had listened to Maynard tell him about Dad setting fire to the packing plant at least once a week since he started at the boat shed. Roy always answered the same. "Dad said he didn't do it, and I believe him. He said he was intending to do it, and that's why he headed back to the plant as soon as it was dark and it was empty. He said he could see through the window that Mr. Cochran was still in his office with the light on. Dad put the coal oil can down and went on back home."

"That's not what the police said," Mr. Whitlock interrupted. "Bill Cochran claimed he wasn't anywhere near the plant."

"Dad says Mr. Cochran burnt it down himself for the insurance. He thinks he saw him outside and afterwards set the plant on fire with Dad's coal oil."

"Yeah, I know that's what Harlow said. At the same time he said he saw it snow on the Fourth of July. You go on over to Milford, Roy, and bring your dad home. I can't pay you for the day, though. Money's tight as beeswax these days. You're going to have to look after Harlow. There's no work around here, you know that. I reckon he can go pick tomatoes and lima beans in season with the colored people, if they'll have him. You can't set fire to a tomato, can you, Maynard?"

Roy closed his ears. Mr. Whitlock was a fair man in spite of what he said against Dad. So was Maynard. The skiffs and rowboats they made in the shed were famous up and down the Chesapeake Bay, people said. Mr. Whitlock's folks had been making boats for over a hundred years. Roy bet they were still using some of them.

The trouble, to be fair, wasn't with them. It was with Dad. He did get drunk once in a while, or he used to—not always like Maynard said, but once in a while when he got paid off at the plant on Saturday. He'd come home rolling from side to side to swear at Mom and slap her once or twice if she talked back and then collapse on the bed. If he remembered the next day, he'd say he was sorry and, like as not, go down to the bus depot which was open on Sunday and come home with a pocket full of Mary Janes, which Mom liked better than other candy bars because they lasted a long time.

Dad hadn't set fire to the plant, Roy was certain. Maybe he meant to, like he said, but he hadn't. Roy could recall Dad coming home from work lots of times, saying that the big new cannery over in Mount Pleasant was buying up all the produce and Cochran's had to take the leftovers. Roy did remember—he was sure—how one night Dad sat right there at the kitchen table with a can of Silver Dime and told Mom and him that he might be out of work pretty soon. Mr. Cochran said he was going to have to close the plant, or burn it down and take the insurance.

Roy later tried to tell the sheriff that, but he didn't pay him any mind. "Go on home now, Roy," he told him. "We'll take care of it." The lawyer Dad had, who was a real drunk, everyone in Tilson knew, told Dad to say he was guilty, because if he didn't and caused the county a lot of trouble on a trial, the judge might put him away for ten years. Arson was a serious business. That's what Dad did. Mom told Roy to stay out of it, that Dad knew what he was doing.

"We'll make it through somehow, Roy," she said. "You'll have to look after Lilian while I go down to the fishhouse. Later maybe you can take a job, too. We'll make it through. Don't you worry none."

They had made it. Except now Mom had taken Lilian and gone away, just like Roy's real mother had done. That time, Dad got Ruth Ann to come in to live, and Roy started to call *her* Mom after she had Lilian and Dad was sent away. Now she was gone, and it would only be Roy and Dad. Well, they would make it, too.

Roy took the sandpaper block and started in on the keelboard. That was the most important board in the whole boat, Mr. Whitlock told him. "Take your time, Roy. It has to be just right. A little too much here or not quite enough there, and the boat will never be right. Remember that, Roy. If you don't get it right at the beginning, they'll have to caulk the boat every spring until they just give up on it and set it loose on the tide to float out to sea and sink. Or else pull it into the marsh and let it rot. I don't ever want one of my boats rotting away in the marsh."

In the evening Mr. Whitlock lifted the keelboard and ran his eye along its length. "It's nice and clean, Roy. You have a good touch. Go on home now and get ready for your father. Here"—Mr. Whitlock reached in his pocket—"buy your ticket with this," he said, handing Roy a dollar bill. "How come you didn't go away with Ruth Ann and Lilian? I heard they left."

Roy looked out over the bay. The wind had shifted and the water was choppy. The tide was running in. Roy could smell the salt water from the ocean. The gulls were wheeling and screeching in the wind. "I don't know exactly," he replied. "I belong here, I guess."

4

"Come to sign Harlow out, have you, Roy? I heard he wanted to stay on we were so good to him," George said. He looked at the clock high on the wall. "I was teasing you, Roy. He'll be along in a minute. Twelve o'clock is checkout time. Unless you're going in the other direction. Then it's whenever the sun comes up. What do you reckon they do on cloudy days?"

Roy moved from foot to foot. He didn't like George's talk about hanging people. He heard steps down the corridor from the other side of the barred door. The door swung open. A guard Roy hadn't seen before stood to one side and let Dad pass on through. He smiled at Roy and gave a hesitant move with his right hand. He clutched a gunnysack in the left.

"You take care, Harlow," George said. "Don't try to set the world on fire." He paused to chuckle at his joke. "You, too, Roy. Look after him for me so I won't have to do it no more."

Harlow straightened up. He took his boy by the shoulder and led him through the front door of the prison and down the walk to the big gate. "Four years," he told Roy slowly, "four years and two months and six days . . . That's a long time, Roy. I could feel myself turning gray in there. I don't ever intend to go back."

"I got our tickets to Tilson," Roy said. He took the two tickets from his shirt pocket to show Dad. "I got mine round-trip. You save ten cents if you buy the round-trip."

His father rubbed a callused hand over Roy's head. "That was good thinking, son. Ten cents will get me a Silver Dime at the café while we wait for the bus."

"Dad, I don't think . . ."

"I was just fooling, Roy. I wanted to see what you'd say. No more drinking for me. I didn't set fire to Cochran's rundown packing plant, but I'd be a fool not to know it was being drunk that night that made it look like I did it."

"You did your time, Dad," Roy said. "Now you're like everybody else again." That was what Mr. Whitlock had said: "Remember this, Roy, Harlow's paid for what he done. He's clean with the law as far as I can see. He's like the rest of us."

"That's not properly so, son. I'd need more than all my fingers to count what the law says I can't do. Ruth Ann will be pleased to hear that drinking is one of them."

When they reached the depot and sat down on the worn wooden bench outside waiting for the bus to come through, Roy's father reached inside the sack. "It's under the dirty shirts," he muttered. "Here it is." He pulled a rag doll out. "Look at her, Roy. I got the buttons on straight this time. I hope Lilian will like her.

15

What do you think?" Harlow's thick fingers tried to smooth out the rope hair that kept curling up. "Her name is Jenny. I didn't stitch it on her apron or anything, but I thought maybe that's what Lilian would like to call her."

This was the moment Roy had been fretting about. He wished Mom had written Dad the note instead of him. He had brought it along in case he couldn't say anything on his own. He fished it out of his pocket. "Mom's gone home to West Virginia," he said, handing his father the crumpled piece of green-lined paper.

His father took the note. He read it silently and gave it back to his son. When the bus rolled in, he stood up with his gunny sack. He put Jenny carefully down on the depot bench, sitting up to wait for someone to come along and take her home. He climbed aboard the bus ahead of Roy and took a seat by the window. He looked out the window all the way to Tilson.

A dirty envelope, "Harlow Purdy" written in a rough hand on the front, was propped against the catsup bottle on the kitchen table. Harlow picked it up and turned it over. "This from Ruth Ann?" he asked Roy.

"You got her letter," Roy reminded Dad. "Anyway, she left on Monday while I was working at the boat shed. That's three days ago."

Harlow ripped the envelope open. Roy could see it was just a couple of lines. His father swore some ugly words and handed the sheet of paper to Roy. "We don't want no arsonis in Tilson," it read. "Go away before we run you off. KKK."

"It's just someone playing a joke, Dad," Roy said.

"Maybe," his father said. "What do we have to eat?"

"Nothing yet," Roy answered. "Mom didn't leave anything. I've been eating bread and cold cuts I brought home after work. I think the ice has run out, too." He looked in the ice chest. "It's all gone. It's not even cool inside."

"I'll go to the store and get us a steak," Harlow said. "I've been dreaming of a big juicy steak the whole time I was gone."

"I'll go, Dad," Roy said. "You sit here and rest. How many pounds of steak? I got money, not much, a little over fifteen dollars. You sit right here. I'll be back."

"Roy, I'm not ashamed of something I didn't do. And I sure as shooting am not going to pay attention to the Klan. If anybody comes around here in a sheet, I'll bust his head open. I don't figure it's them anyway. It's just somebody who knows how to put three K's in a row on a piece of paper. And I have my money, too. You get the frying pan out and start some kindling in the stove. We'll have us a banquet."

Roy watched his father stalk out of the house. His shoulders were all the way back now. He walked with purpose. Dad was a proud man, Roy thought. He had gone through high school and a year of Chesapeake College before he left to marry. That was when his troubles began, he used to say. He wouldn't take an ordinary job, and there weren't any good jobs around. Roy guessed that was when he started drinking Saturday nights. He remembered Ma threatening to leave if he kept on, and she did.

Ma had been to high school with Dad, studying secretarial sciences, and wasn't about to spend the rest of her life in a four-room shack on the edge of a stinking marsh, she said. "I can't take care of Roy where I'm going," she told her husband. "I won't have anyone to leave him with. If I find I can take care of you, honey, I'll be straight back to get you."

"That means she's going over to Baltimore," Harlow told him. "Shirley's always wanted to work in the city." They waited for her to write or come back to see them, but Ma never did, and after a while they didn't wait anymore.

5

Dad didn't come back to the house right away. Roy sat on the back stoop, on the step that had sprung loose, and waited. The shack was propped up on cinder blocks about twenty steps from the marsh, which did smell bad at low tide. The outhouse was perched on a couple of more cinder blocks practically in the marsh. When the moon was full on a northeast wind, the tide sometimes came up right under the floor of the outhouse.

Dad wasn't walking straight when he cut off the county road onto the weedy path down to the shack. He wasn't rolling from side to side, so Roy guessed he hadn't yet had too much to drink. He carried a paper bag in one arm, and as he came closer, Roy could see he had a brown bottle in the other.

He nodded to Roy who stood to one side and held the ratty screen door open for Dad to pass inside. He followed and poked up the fire. He took some sections of creosoted planks from the pile of driftwood he had collected from the edge of the marsh. The creosoted boards burned like crazy. He put the tin frying pan on top of the stove.

"Here's the steak, Roy," Dad said. He took a blood-soaked package from the bag. "And I got us a bag of potato chips and some devil's food cupcakes. We'll have a real celebration. I'll have my steak rare, like your mother used to cook it. Ruth Ann always thought she had to cook it through."

Harlow reached inside the bag and brought out another bottle of beer. "I kept thinking in the prison about the steak and that started me thinking about National Bohemian. It's made right here in the state, over in Baltimore, not hauled halfway across the country. You can tell that it's a local beer."

The bottom of the pan was red hot. Roy wrapped a dish towel around the handle and lifted the pan off the stove. He waited a moment, then dropped the meat in the pan. It sizzled, giving off a smell charred meat did. He put the pan back on the range and took a fork from the kitchen table drawer. He counted to a hundred and turned the steak over. He counted again, cut two-thirds of it off, and put it on a plate for Dad. He let his portion cook awhile longer.

Roy shook the potato chip crumbs into his hand and licked them up. His father had finished and was leaning back, his feet on Mom's empty chair. He prized the cap off another bottle of beer. "That was real good, Roy," he said, "every bit as good as I thought it would be. Like this bottle of beer. It costs a nickel more, but it's twice as good as Silver Dime, I can tell you."

"You're not supposed to be drinking, are you, Dad?"

"That's what Sheriff Rother told me in town not more

than an hour ago. 'Who says I'm drinking, Sheriff?' I said straight back. 'I'm buying.' He didn't care about that, anyway. He had something else on his mind."

"What was that?" Roy asked.

"He had seen me go into the American Store from the jail window, he said, and he came across the street to have a talk. Right there at the counter in front of everyone. There were a lot of people in Tilson, he said, who had taken out fire insurance. He gave me an envelope. 'It's in here,' he said."

"'What's this?'" I said.

"'You might call it a donation, Harlow. Folks don't want you in town; they took up a collection to help you on your way. It ain't much, but as one of them said, Harlow Purdy ain't worth much either.'"

Roy watched his father empty the envelope on the table. Some coins rolled onto the floor, where the boy picked them up. With thick fingers, Harlow counted the bills and coins. "Thirteen dollars and forty-six cents. That's not much for a grown man and a boy. They gave Judas more than that. Well, I reckon we'll take it anyway."

"Are you going away?" Roy asked in disbelief.

"*We* are going away. That's what I bought the beer for. I'm not drinking anymore after tonight, but I've lived here in town all my life, except for four years, and it seemed right to celebrate my leaving. I drank a couple on the way home to get my courage up to tell you."

"But, Dad, I have a job. Next year Mr. Whitlock is making me a boat builder. It's enough for us until you get a job, too, Dad. I can't leave the Bay. I would have gone with Mom if I wanted to leave. She said you'd start

21

drinking the minute you got out," Roy told his father resentfully. "She was right."

"I bet she also said I wouldn't be able to get a job."

"Yes," Roy murmured.

"She was right again. It's time for us to move on, Roy. This is no place for a man to get up in the world. Put your things in the canvas bag, if Ruth Ann left it behind. I have a good job waiting for me a long ways from here. You can go to school there, too. You don't want to be a river rat all your life. Go on and pack. I have something to do."

6

Roy didn't have much to pack: his winter boots, the sweater Mom gave him for Christmas, some dirty shirts and underwear he hadn't got around to washing, and an extra pair of pants. And the bone-handled pocket-knife Mr. Whitlock said he could have. The man whose job Roy filled in for had left his knife behind. When he didn't come back to claim it, Mr. Whitlock gave it to Roy. "There's not a better knife made," he told Roy.

He stuffed his wallet into his hip pocket and buttoned the flap over it. His jacket, where was his jacket? He found it hanging to the side of Mom's closet. She had washed and ironed it and put it away for the fall. Roy slipped it over his shoulders. He wondered whether it was hot or cold where they were going.

Then he stood, uncertain about leaving, in the empty room where Mom and Lilian had slept. It wasn't right, he thought. The day Dad got out of jail he took it in his head to leave. He didn't even tell Roy where. Were they walking? Dad had said it was a long ways off, so they might be taking the bus—or the train. It was too late for the train. It made only two trips a day up the shore from Tilson, one in the middle of the morning and the other in the middle of the afternoon.

It had to be the bus, he figured. It came by this time of the evening and went all the way up to where you could catch another bus to go to Baltimore. On still nights, he could hear it out on the state highway when the driver stopped to pick somebody up and then started off again.

Roy thought of Mr. Whitlock. He couldn't just go off without telling him, not after he gave him the whole day off to go meet Dad. There was Mom's notepaper and envelopes in the kitchen cabinet. He could write Mr. Whitlock a note and put it in the mailbox.

The fumes of coal oil seeped into the bedroom. They were strong. What was Dad doing? Roy went out into the kitchen. His father was splashing coal oil over the kitchen floor. He lifted the can up to douse the icebox and the cabinet and the table. When he saw Roy, he put the can down on the chair.

"You ready, Roy? Let's be on our way, before it evaporates." Harlow put the wadded dishtowel to the spout of the can and soaked it. He pushed his son out of the kitchen. "Go stand next to my gunnysack away from the stoop. She'll go up in a rush when she starts."

Roy watched. It was almost dark. The days were getting shorter, he thought idly. His father backed out of the kitchen. Holding the screen door open with his backside, Harlow struck a wooden match on the side of the shack. He held it to the dishtowel. When it flared up, he tossed it underhand into the room. He let the screen door spring shut and came to stand beside his son.

"We'll wait until we're sure she goes up. She ought to. The can was almost full. You must not have used the heater much last winter."

"We ran out. Soon as I had the can filled, it turned warm and never did get cold again," Roy told his father. He waited to see the shack flame up.

"That's what always happens," his father said. "You prepare for something, then it doesn't happen, and you have gone and wasted your time and money. Like me going to college for a year. It didn't do me a whit of good. There she goes now, Roy, it's spreading."

Through the door they could see the flames flicker higher. The doll! Roy had put Mary Jane on the top kitchen shelf. He dropped the canvas bag and before his father could stop him, he dashed up the steps into the kitchen. He ran around the edge of the flames to the cabinet. He reached for the doll. She was at the back of the shelf. He stood on tiptoe. He heard the fire crackling and felt its heat on his back. "Roy," his father shouted through door. "Get out of there!"

He had her. The boy turned and jumped once, twice, over the flames to the door. Smoke in his eyes, he stumbled down the steps into the yard. The scorched hair on his arms smelled like the charred steak.

"What the hell did you think you were doing?" Harlow demanded.

"I don't know," the boy explained. "I had a sudden thought about Mary Jane, and it didn't seem right to burn her up, too." He bent over to stuff the rag doll into his bag. He might see Lilian someday and she might take to Mary Jane and not care that her eyes weren't on straight.

Harlow shook his head in wonderment. He put his arm around Roy's shoulders. The shack was ablaze. The breeze off the bay drew the smoke and fiery cinders high into the evening sky. Roy shuddered as he watched. The shack was all he knew growing up; even though it wasn't much to live in, he felt sad. Later on the shack would be all he would have to think back to.

"Let's go on out to the highway," Roy said. The volunteer fire truck would be along shortly, as soon as the fire was high enough to be seen in town. He didn't want to be around when Mr. Whitlock and Maynard, both of them volunteers, showed up.

Father and son turned away from the shack. Flames were licking up through the tarpaper roof. "I hadn't oughtn't to have done that," Harlow said, "but I had to. Frank Cochran owed me a burning for the lies he told that put me away for four years. I reckon he don't have insurance on the place. I hope not. I don't remember how much I owed him. Did Ruth Ann keep the payments up, all of them?"

"We only missed one," Roy replied, "when Lilian had to go to the doctor for an infection. Mr. Cochran said we better get it to him by the next period, or he'd have to take measures."

Harlow stopped for a minute. His lips moved as

he did his calculations. "Almost eight years we were paying for the old wreck and before that I was paying rent. I figure I still owe him upwards of five hundred dollars. Well, he can sing for it now, can't he, Roy? It's not likely he'll come all the way to California to collect."

7

The bus lumbered to a stop, and the driver pushed the door open. "It looks like a fire over there toward the bay. What do you reckon it is?"

"Couldn't tell you," Harlow answered. "How much do you want?"

"How far you going?" the driver asked.

"All the way up the shore."

"From Tilson," the driver said to himself. "Let's see." He peered in the dim light at a piece of cardboard. "One way?" he asked.

"One way, all the way," Roy heard his father say happily.

"That's two dollars and twenty cents each."

Harlow took a small roll of bills from his pocket. He found a five-dollar bill. He stuffed the change in his pocket. "Let's find us a couple of good seats, Roy," he said. "You can sit by the window if you want."

"How long is it?" Roy asked the driver.

"It's a long trip, sonny. If we keep to the schedule it's

about six hours. You'll get there in the middle of the night."

Roy went halfway down the aisle where Dad stood waiting. He slipped into the seat by the window. This bus wasn't like the rattly local bus that took him over to Milford. Here he had a plush seat and a little metal pocket for an ashtray. He leaned forward as the bus started up and pulled out onto the highway. Through the window on the other side, where an old couple was sitting, you could see the flames reaching into the evening sky. "Looks like a real bad fire, Mother," the old man said to his wife. "I hope there's nobody inside."

"Look here, Roy," his father said. "You can push your seat back. Isn't that something?" He showed the boy a button on the side of the seat. "You push the button and lean back at the same time. You can take a real snooze on this bus."

Roy let the seat back. The window at his side was half open. The warm air of the summer evening poured in, touched with the salty smell of the tide. Roy breathed deeply. He wouldn't be smelling the Chesapeake Bay for a while. And he hadn't written the letter to Mr. Whitlock to tell him he was going away. He and Maynard would probably figure it out for themselves when they came to put out the fire. He had a sudden frightening thought.

"Do you reckon they'll think we're inside?" he asked his father.

Dad was leaning back in his seat, eyes closed, almost asleep. Beer always made him sleepy. "What?" he murmured.

"Do you think the volunteers will look for us in the shack?" Roy asked in a low voice. He didn't want the old couple across the aisle to hear.

Dad opened his eyes. "I hadn't thought of it, Roy. They won't find us, will they? I reckon Frank Cochran will figure it out soon enough. I wouldn't worry about it, son. Why don't you stretch back like me and take a nap. There's no telling how it will be when we head west. You know, Roy, I'm almost forty years old, and I have never been out of the state, except down the bottom of the shore that belongs to Virginia. By rights it belongs to Maryland, they say."

He might as well find out where they were going while Dad was still awake, Roy thought. He knew where California was, all the way across the country. He had been in school long enough to learn the map of the U.S.A. Mr. Whitlock had taken his wife across the country in his new 1935 Chrysler the year before Roy went to work at the boat shed. He was still talking about how long it took and how hot it was in the desert. "I spit in the Pacific Ocean," he told Maynard. "They had this long pier out onto the water, like at Ocean City, and Mother and I walked out and I leaned over the railing where they were fishing and spit. Mother wanted to know what I did that for. I told her it was because I wanted to, so I could say I spit in the Pacific Ocean like that Spanish explorer in the history books."

Maynard always replied, "Did you hit anything?" Then Mr. Whitlock and Maynard would laugh and go back to work.

"Where are we going, Dad? I mean, where in California?"

Harlow reached in his shirt pocket. He unfolded a slip of paper. He leaned over to read what it said by the little aisle light on the outside of his seat. He couldn't make out the writing. "I can't read it in the dark, but I remember that it's in some part of Los Angeles."

"You have a job waiting for you?" Roy asked. That didn't seem likely to him, somehow. Who out in California was going to hire someone fresh out of jail?

Harlow sensed his son's doubts. "Not a job waiting specifically for me, just a job I'd most likely get if I showed up and asked for one."

"What kind of job, Dad?"

"Security work. That sounds kind of farfetched, I know, but that's what Jack O'Neill said, 'security work.'"

"Jack O'Neill?" Was Dad talking about one of the guards who used to patrol the visiting room to keep people from trying to touch through the wire mesh? He took Dad's shirts and cupcakes and westerns and promised to deliver them as soon as the visit was over. The last year or so, another guard had taken his place. "Are you talking about Mr. O'Neill, the guard?" Roy asked.

"That's Jack. He was good to me in there. He'd slip me a can of beer for the regular price, not fifty cents the way the other ones did. He quit and went out to California where his brother-in-law has a security company that hires out guards to factories and banks and the like. He told me to look him up if I decided to leave the Shore. 'They can always use a big strong man like you, Harlow. You don't have to tell them you did some time.' He gave me this address."

"A policeman?" Roy asked. "They'll make you a policeman?"

"Not a proper one, a guard I guess you could call me. I thought about it the last year. It didn't take any brains to figure out I wasn't going to get myself hired close to home. I thought I'd gather you and Ruth Ann and the baby up and go to California to start over. It might be my last chance. Things are bound to be different out west."

"Are you going to write Ruth Ann to join us?" Roy asked.

"I can't rightly say, Roy. It looks like she doesn't want to be with me anymore. We'll have to wait to see how things turn out, won't we?"

Harlow put his head back and shut his eyes. Roy turned his face to the breeze streaming through the half-opened window.

8

Harlow nudged Roy as the bus rolled into the depot. "It's the end of the line," he said. "Now, we'll start heading west."

Roy rubbed his eyes and stretched. He remembered the button at the side of his seat. He pushed it and the back of the seat pressed forward. He pulled the window down and shivered. There was a chill in the night air. When he looked around, the bus was empty.

"Where are all the people?" he asked. The bus had been half-filled when they boarded outside of Tilson.

"They all got off along the way. We must have made thirty to forty stops, picking folks up and dropping them off. I couldn't figure out where they were all going this late in the evening."

As they stepped down from the bus, the driver wished them good luck. "It's a long way to California," he said. "I took the Greyhound out there—I got a ticket for half price—and it seemed like we would never arrive. Five days it took, I seem to recollect. But it's interesting to see this big country. It changes all the time as you go along. Well, I'm going to sleep awhile. Toward dawn I start back down the road."

The waiting room was empty. The man behind the ticket window nodded, eyes half-closed. Beyond the patch of light in the depot, the town was dark. In the distance Roy could see a single street light. He guessed it was Main Street.

Harlow ran his tongue around his lips. His mouth was dry. "No place in town open this late?" he asked the man.

The agent made a show of looking over his shoulder at the clock on the wall. "The diner closes at ten or thereabouts. The bar in the Howard Hotel shuts down at midnight. There's a cooler outside if you have a mind for a soft drink. Not much goes on around here after the picture show lets out. That's about the only thing that goes on around here, anyway, 'cept for bingo in the armory Wednesday nights. Where you two men headed for?"

"Los Angeles, California," Roy heard his father say. "We'd like two tickets to Los Angeles. Can you take care of that for us?"

"I sure can," the agent said, paying attention now. "I don't get many calls for tickets all the way to California. Let's see what we have here." He opened a book about as thick as the Montgomery Ward catalogue Ruth Ann kept in her bureau drawer and had taken with her to West Virginia. "We'll get you to Chicago first. Most all the buses go through Chicago. That's the easy part. Lots of people go to Chicago for some reason. Okay. The bus from Washington comes through about five o'clock— that's two hours—and carries you to Pittsburgh. That's not an express bus, you understand. But I can put you

34

on an express bus from there to Chicago. Out of the Windy City, there's a through bus to Los Angeles."

"You mean no changes?" Harlow asked. "She goes right on through?"

"Yep, all the way. Of course you stop regular along the way and you can get off to eat and go to the bathroom, but you climb back onto the seats you had. No one can take them while you're outside. Greyhound put this special bus on just last year."

Harlow reached in his pocket. He looked pleased. "Did you hear that, Roy? It's a special bus. Does the express cost more?" he asked. "We don't have much money."

"I don't think so. I'll check and add it up for you. Round-trip or one-way? You save 10 percent round-trip."

"One way. We're not counting on coming back soon."

The ticket agent added up figures on a scrap of paper. "Two one-way tickets to Los Angeles, California. That's forty-seven dollars and eighty cents each. Too bad the boy isn't under twelve. He could go half fare. No way, now. How old are you, son?"

"Fourteen, almost fifteen."

"And you're big for your age, too. I'm sorry I have to charge full fare. Money's tight these days."

Roy's father took the bills out of his pocket. He counted them out on the shelf in front of the ticket window. He looked puzzled. He reached deep in the right pocket, then into the left pocket and then two hip pockets. He counted the money another time, looking carefully at each bill. He turned around to Roy in confusion. "I had more than this. There were two twenty-dollar bills. The rest was fives and ones." He reached up to the two pockets of his faded denim shirt. "What's the total come to again?" he asked with an embarrassed smile.

"Ninety-five dollars and sixty cents."

"I have to talk to my boy," Harlow said.

"Take your time," the agent said. He took a magazine from under the counter and began to turn the pages. It seemed to Roy he was trying to make up for his father's embarrassment.

"I don't understand it, Roy. They gave me a hundred and thirty dollars they owed me for the work I did while I was inside. It was more, but they took out for a lot of things they shouldn't have taken out for. They counted it out right in front of me. It was all there. Two twenty-dollar bills and lots of little ones. It felt good rolled up in my pocket. Now the two twenties are gone."

"How much do you have now?" Roy asked. Maybe if Dad couldn't buy the tickets, they could go back home. They could rent another place. There were a couple of old shacks along the marsh they could fix up. Places that hadn't been lived in for a long time, with leaky roofs and the windows out. They probably didn't even have owners. Dad could fix one up while he went back to the boat shed.

Harlow counted the money in his pocket for the third time. "Ninety-three dollars thereabouts, counting the thirteen dollars the sheriff gave me. It's almost enough, but we have to have some money for ourselves."

Harlow counted one more time. "I know what likely happened, Roy. They gave me the two twenties first and piled the other bills on top. I think they must have slipped to the floor when I took out the roll to pay for the bus ticket. It was almost dark, and I wasn't being too careful. And they blew right out the door. Well, there's no help for it. I'm determined to go to California, one way or another. How much money do you have in your wallet, Roy?"

"Fifteen dollars I saved from my wages." Roy realized he had to go with Dad. He had a feeling he was going to need him along the way. Losing forty dollars after he had drunk the beer, you could see Dad wasn't used to being out of prison yet. "The train would be a whole lot more, wouldn't it?" he asked.

"I think so. We'll ask the ticket man."

The agent slipped the magazine under the counter. "Oh, yes," he said. "Maybe twice as much. You can't beat Greyhound for getting you there cheap."

Harlow straightened his shoulders the way he did when he walked through the prison gates a free man. "What's done is done. I should have been more careful. Let's figure it out, Roy. You keep your money for an emergency. I won't feel right using it unless we have to. We'll put some money aside to buy sandwiches with as we go along. That will leave us seventy-five dollars to go on. Does that sound right?" Harlow asked.

Roy didn't answer. He wondered what Dad was going to do with seventy-five dollars.

"How far can we go on this?" Harlow asked, pushing most of his bills under the grill. It's seventy-five dollars."

The ticket agent studied the pile of money. "It's cheaper the farther you go, you understand. Not altogether cheaper, but cheaper by the mile. Let me see." He studied his book again. "The best I can do is Wichita. That's seventy-three dollars and ninety cents."

"Wichita? Where's that at?"

"It's in Kansas. You'd be over halfway to California."

"We'll do that, Roy!" Harlow said with determination. "We'll stop over and work our way west. It will take longer, but that's what we'll do."

"These are tough times, Mister," the agent said. "I wouldn't count on finding much work out there. I hear their farms are blowing away out there and folks are packing up and going to California, just like you. It's none of my business, of course, but I thought I'd better tell you before you went ahead and bought tickets. That wouldn't be right."

"That's our problem," Harlow said. "Grown men can decide these matters for themselves, can't we, Roy? Anyway," he told the agent, "we have kind of burnt our bridges behind us."

9

Roy and his father stumbled from the bus in Wichita. Harlow stretched and rolled his head to loosen the muscles. "That was really something," he complained. "Four whole days and nights cramped into those narrow seats, listening to babies yell and choking half to death on cigar smoke. Remember that one bus we had for a stretch outside of Chicago? It didn't even have seats that pushed back. It was just like those old buses that run from Tilson down to the cape."

Roy didn't need to be reminded. It had been a hot, sweaty trip all the way. Most of the time he didn't have a seat by the window. One part of the ride there were so many people on the bus he had to stand up in the back in the colored section. Now he walked to the edge of the platform. A long dusty street went past the station in both directions. To the right were buildings and stores and traffic lights. An occasional car drove by. To the left, out toward the country, were big silos—really big silos—and fenced-in fields. He breathed in deeply. He felt the dust in his throat and tasted it in his mouth. He sniffed the smell of manure in the air. It seemed he could hear the lowing of cattle in the distance.

Harlow joined him and handed Roy his bag. He pointed toward the silos and the fences. "That's where they keep the corn, in those silos, and the cattle they ship in here from the range, a man in the bus was telling me. They feed them up for a while and ship them on into Chicago. Do you reckon that steak we had the night we left came through here? Wichita isn't much to look at, is it? We better go find us a boardinghouse to sleep in. It will be getting dark in a while. Can you make it without supper tonight, Roy? I'm down to my last five-dollar bill. We'll get a job tomorrow and start to eat regular again. But it won't be ham sandwiches, I can tell you that."

"That's okay," Roy said. "I'm not all that hungry. Where are you going to find a boardinghouse?"

Pointing to the right, his father said, "Let's walk in that direction. If we go the other way, we'll end up sleeping with the cattle."

At six-thirty most of the stores were closed. It was stifling, unbearably hot as Roy and Harlow trudged along with their bags. A few farmers, old men with sad eyes and wrinkled cheeks, leaned forward on the steps of the hardware store, gnarled hands wrapped around their knees. One of them nodded to Roy. "Evening, son," he said in a strange flat accent that Roy had never heard before.

A drugstore was open at the street corner. Inside he saw two ceiling fans turning. He was thirsty. "Let's have a Dr Pepper, Dad, I'll pay for it. We can find out inside about a place to sleep."

"You were going to save your money, Roy," his father said. "We can find some water."

"It's only twenty cents, Dad. It's an emergency."

Two couples were seated in high wire-backed chairs down at the end of the counter. The boys had soft drinks, and the girls were sharing a milkshake through two straws. "You have Dr Pepper?" Roy asked.

"Only in a bottle," the man behind the counter told him. "If you want a fountain drink, we have Coca-Cola, root beer, and cherry."

"A bottle is okay." Roy unbuttoned his hip pocket and took out his wallet. He lifted out a dollar bill. When he received the change, he put it in the coin pocket and snapped it shut. He put the wallet back in his trousers and buttoned the flap tight.

"Where you folks from?" the man asked.

"The Eastern Shore," Roy said proudly.

The man was puzzled. "Where's that at?"

"Back East," Roy's father replied. "In Maryland. On a piece of land between the bay and the ocean. They call it the Eastern Shore."

"I just never heard of it. Where you headed?"

Roy answered again. "California."

"Well, you ain't alone. Seems like half the state is taking off for California. Like in the days of the big gold rush. Only I hear there's no gold out there, now. Hard work if you can find it and no pay."

"I have a job waiting for me," Roy's father said. "We got off the bus this evening when our money gave out, except for the boy's emergency money. I won't let him spend that. If a man can't look after his boy, he probably

41

can't look after himself either. We figure on working our way out to California from here."

"Good luck. Maybe I'll go with you. Mr. Wilson—he owns the drugstore—says he can't keep me on after the end of the month. He's going to do the counter and the prescriptions himself. I don't know rightly what I'm going to do. I had a job in the cattle yards for twelve years—until last spring when most of us were laid off. Not much coming through these days."

"There aren't any pickup jobs around?" Harlow asked. "We aren't particular. Something to get my boy and me back on the bus for a couple of hundred miles."

"This time of year used to be you could get a job anywhere, but . . ." The man paused to look out the window. "It's the drought and the dust storms. The silos are empty. The corn in the field doesn't grow a foot high. Then it curls up and dies. Out there on Main Street it's empty. Nobody at the picture show or the cafés and bars."

"It looks like we'll have to hoof it, Roy," Harlow said. "Maybe we can catch a ride on the highway."

"You'd be better off riding the rails. That's what the men do, even some of the women; they catch a freight going west out of the yards and hope they can make a hundred miles or more before the bulls catch them. They get thrown off and start over again. The thing is, some of those railroad men with clubs like to use them. You have to be careful."

Seeing that Roy and his father didn't understand, the man leaned on the counter. "It works like this," he began. He stopped to gather up the two empty bottles and put them under the counter. He replaced them with two fresh bottles. He lifted the cover from the custard pie and cut two large pieces. He put a plate and a fork in front of Roy and Harlow. "Mr. Wilson's off to supper. He don't have to learn about this. He often does the same himself. Anyway, the custard pie will be spoiled by tomorrow. It turns bad fast in this heat.

"What you do if you have a mind to try it is to go to the railroad yards toward dark. They unload the cattle cars and make up a train to go back west. When it starts to pull out, folks pile in. The cars don't smell so good, and I hear it gets cold at night, but it's free. You'd best jump out when you see the train is going to stop. If the bulls catch you, they'll beat you up. But there's so many people riding, they can't catch everyone. Even if they do, the jails don't want them because they have to feed them."

"There are no jobs in town, you're sure?" Harlow asked.

"Mister, if I knew of a job in town, I wouldn't be telling you. I'd take it for myself. There's always someone at the tracks to tell you what to do. Some of those men are real hoboes; all they do is ride back and forth across the country for the plain heck of it."

Harlow turned to his son. "What do you think, Roy? It beats walking."

Roy didn't quite understand what the man behind the counter said, but it sounded exciting. He swallowed the last piece of pie and washed it down with Dr Pepper. "Sure," he said.

10

The man came from behind the counter to the front door of the drugstore. "Go past the stoplight," he instructed Harlow, "and down two blocks. Cross the street and go three blocks until you come to Sycamore Street. Go right half a block and you'll see the sign, Sycamore House. Tell Mrs. Franklin I sent you. She won't charge you any more than the others that rent rooms, and they might be a lot cleaner. I calculate it will be a dollar a night for the room. If you decide to take the train, be sure to wait until it's almost dark. Otherwise, you might get your head cracked open. Good luck to you." He held out his hand, first to Roy, then to Harlow. "Maybe I'll see you out in California one of these days. I sure ain't got any future in Kansas."

Sycamore was a street of large frame houses. It was a little cooler under the trees, but you could feel the heat lying heavy all around. The branches were motionless, covered with a pale whitish dust. There were few lights to be seen in the houses they passed. An old couple was rocking on the front porch of one house, just rocking

back and forth, sort of in time, without looking street-
ward to see who was passing by.

"Everyone must be inside," Harlow said. "It's bound
to be cooler inside if you keep the shades down and
don't let the hot air in. Makes you wish you were back
on the bay with your face in the breeze, doesn't it?" He
stopped in front of a neat white sign hanging on a post.
"Sycamore House," Harlow said. "We had the directions
right."

Father and son went up the three steps and across the
porch to a heavy wooden door with a little window of
thick glass you couldn't see through. Harlow pulled the
brass knob beside the door. Inside, a bell tinkled. They
waited for the sound of steps approaching.

"They must not of heard," Roy said to his father.
"Could I try this time?"

Harlow nodded. He pushed his felt hat back on his
head and wiped his brow with his hand. Roy noticed that
Dad looked older. The hair above his ears was turning
gray, and his eyes were tired and sad, like the old men's
on the steps of the hardware store. The stretch in the
penitentiary hadn't done him any good. He didn't seem
as confident as he used to be, even when everything was
going wrong. I better get him to California pretty soon,
Roy thought. He gave the brass knob a long, impatient
pull.

Before the echo of the bell died, a voice called, "I'm
coming. Just hold on."

The heavy oak door swung open. A tall, gaunt woman
in a housecoat and felt slippers stood in the doorway.
"Yes?" she said.

"A man in the drugstore out on Main Street said you

had rooms to let," Harlow asked. "We'd be obliged if you let us spend the night. We're passing through on our way west," Harlow said.

"They chased you off down at the freight yards?" the woman asked. "I can't figure out why they can't give you folks a helping hand."

"No, ma'am," Harlow explained. "We came in on the bus this afternoon. We're almost out of money. We might have to take the freight tomorrow night."

"You and the boy?"

"Yes, ma'am. We're together. Roy is my son."

"Come on in. I have plenty of rooms free. Next, you're going to tell me you can't pay."

Roy saw his father pause. Before he could answer, Roy spoke up. "No, ma'am. We don't want charity. We have money to pay for the room, if it's not too much. It's just that we don't have money to pay the bus and our food, too." He reached in his pocket and took out Dad's old wallet to show the woman.

"Put your money away, son. It's a dollar for the room if you can spare it. Have you had your supper?"

"A piece of pie at the drugstore," Harlow said. "We'll be all right, thank you, ma'am."

"Clem gave you the pie, I bet. No wonder Mr. Wilson's letting him go. He feeds everyone who walks in."

"We didn't ask," Roy said. "We paid for our Dr Pepper and while we were talking he put a plate down in front of us. But we didn't ask."

"No need to be so touchy proud, son," the woman said. "If someone gives you something these days, it's because they are able to do it and want you to have it.

You can bet the bankers and politicians aren't going to look after you. President Roosevelt learned that quick enough. He must have said to himself, 'I'm going to have to do it all myself.' Come on back to the kitchen."

The woman opened the door of a shiny white refrigerator with a beehive sitting on top. "I have cottage cheese and homemade apple sauce and a couple of cold chops Dad didn't finish last night. Will that do you?"

"Yes, ma'am," Harlow said. "Can we wash our hands at your sink?"

"Go right ahead. There's a fresh roller towel on your left. Dad's out on an emergency call. He's a lineman with the power company. A twister left some lines down in the next county. I don't reckon he'll be home tonight. He'll go to sleep in the truck when he gives out. I don't complain. He's got a job and I thank the Lord for that. You folks are from back East?"

"Maryland, the Eastern Shore part, not Baltimore. That's on the other side of the bay. People have heard of Baltimore, but not much of the Eastern Shore."

"Things aren't any better there, I suppose, or you and the boy wouldn't be out here, would you?"

"If they are, they didn't tell me about it," Harlow replied. "A friend of mine promised me a job in California, but he didn't send the money to get there. We better go off to bed, Roy. We'll look for a job tomorrow. After that, we'll see."

Roy took a dollar from his wallet. He gave it to Mrs. Franklin, who folded it and dropped it into a coffee can on the shelf under the cupboard. She led them to an oaken staircase, a faded runner on the steps, and then down a hall to the rear of the house.

"The rooms to the back are a mite cooler," she said. "A breeze might spring up toward dawn if you want to have the window open. The bathroom is down the hall on your right."

"You shouldn't have offered to pay, Roy," his father said. "We're going to need your money pretty soon. Her husband has a job, like she says."

"We should pay while we can, Dad. When we don't have any money, we'll not pay then. Doesn't that seem right to you?"

Harlow didn't answer. "That bed looks good," he said in a tired voice. "You want right or left?"

"I don't care," Roy said. He dropped his bag at the foot of the bed and slipped out of his shoes, shirt, and pants. He fell into the bed. Before Harlow could turn out the light overhead, Roy was asleep.

11

After four nights in the bus, it seemed to Roy that he had never slept in a bed before. He awoke slowly, bunched up on his side and a little bit chilly. A gentle breeze was blowing the white gauze curtain at the bedroom window. He stumbled to the bathroom. He held up the smelly clothes he had been wearing since they left Tilson, then dropped them and put on his last clean shirt and underwear and went downstairs.

Dad was standing at the kitchen door, looking outside. "Mrs. Franklin is going to wash our clothes for us, Roy, and hang them on the line in the backyard with her own. There's some coffee on the stove. Cut yourself some bread. We can use up the jar of damson preserves, she said."

Roy sat at the table and cut himself a slab of the white bread. He was hungry. His father went to the counter to pick up Mrs. Franklin's Chase and Sanborn coffee can. His hand reached inside. It came out holding a wad of dollar bills.

"Look at this, Roy. Isn't it something, all these bills

folded up in there? There must be a hundred of them, at least. I'd counted up to seventy-four, when Mrs. Franklin came in for more clothespins, and there were still some left at the bottom."

"That's her room money," Roy said. "She must keep it apart from her spending money." He felt uneasy to see Dad handling Mrs. Franklin's savings.

"Do you reckon she'd care too much if we were to borrow a few of these little darlings to help us along to California?"

Roy looked at his father in astonishment. Mrs. Franklin had fed them supper and breakfast and was washing their dirty clothes. She would even have given them the room for nothing, if he hadn't spoken up last night.

"What I mean to say, Roy, is that her old man has a job, and she just takes in boarders for the heck of it. President Roosevelt says we have to share the wealth these days." Harlow laughed uneasily at his son's silence.

"That's stealing, Dad. We can't do that. You must have seen men in the prison who were there for stealing, robbing banks, or something, like John Dillinger."

"It's not the same, Roy. This isn't a bank, and your father's not John Dillinger. Anyway, Mrs. Franklin wouldn't tell on us. We'd be long gone by the time she discovered ten dollars or so was missing. Plus your money, we could take the bus practically to California. I think we ought to do it."

When Harlow began to count out the bills, Roy pushed his chair back. He took the money from his father's hands and put it in the can. He shoved the can into the corner of the cupboard. Then he took the wallet from his pocket. "We can't do it, Dad. They must have done something to you in the prison to make you want to steal. Here is ten dollars of my boat-shed money. You take charge of it. We'll be all right, Dad. We're going to be fine without Mrs. Franklin's money. Let's drink up our coffee and go find a job. If we're lucky, we'll find something and stay on here until we make our tickets to California."

Mrs. Franklin came in from the backyard, wiping her hands on her apron. "You got up, did you, Roy? You must have been real tuckered out. Four days on a bus, I don't know that I could stand that, all cooped up. I have to keep moving around. Dad says I'm one of those perpetual motion machines. I'll wear out someday, I tell him, and who's going to look after you then? The sun's out bright. It's going to be another scorcher. The clothes will be dry soon, if you have a mind to keep on moving."

"We'll go see if we can find something here to do," Harlow said. "Roy was saying we might stay on for a while, if you'll have us."

"I'd like to have you, but you two aren't going to be finding jobs anywhere in Wichita, or even in the whole state of Kansas. We are in the worst depression in the history of the United States, folks keep saying."

"Where should we be looking, ma'am?"

"The Lord knows. If Dad was here, he might have some ideas. The stockyards mostly, I suppose. There's no point in talking to the grain companies, their silos are empty. There haven't been any crops the last two years. You know where the cattle yards are, don't you?"

"Yes, ma'am. We'll be off now," Harlow said. He drained his coffee and rinsed the cups at the sink.

"You don't have a hat, do you, Roy?" Mrs. Franklin asked.

"No, ma'am, but I'll be all right."

"Nobody's all right in a Kansas summer sun without a hat on his head. I'll get you one of Dad's old hats from the closet. He won't care none." Mrs. Franklin returned with a farmer's straw hat, which she put squarely on Roy's head. "Would you look at that, a perfect fit. See yourself in the mirror over there, Roy."

At the stockyards a long line of men stretched into the road in front of a wooden building. "Is this where the work is?" Harlow asked the last man in line, a tall young man in farm overalls and cracked work boots.

"Not for us. I overslept, and here I am at the end. They won't take more than the first ten or twelve men, unless it's a long train."

"What's the work like?" Roy asked.

"Cleaning out the cattle cars and hosing them down after they get the steer off. Three dollars for a day's work if you get it. It's a dirty job. You end up smelling like the cattle, my wife says."

"How come there's so many waiting when they only take ten men?" Harlow asked.

"For the same reason you're here. It's the only job there is. Nothing else to do, except wait in line. You'll see when the time comes that the line will move a little bit. The rest of us will keep on waiting. You never know. Another train or two might come in today. At the end of the day, we all go home, but we'll be back tomorrow."

An hour later, anticipation spread along the line. A train had come in. Roy could hear the bellowing of the cattle as they were unloaded. After another hour, a man appeared at the door of the building, a clipboard in his hand. "We need twelve men. The usual, three dollars. Come sign up if you're interested."

The men at the head of the line raced to the steps. Those behind them shuffled forward. The line seemed as long as it was before. No one spoke.

In the middle of the afternoon, another train pulled into the stockyards. Roy stood on tiptoe to count the cars as they passed. Sixty-two. That meant, he guessed, that they would only take another eight to ten men. "What do you think, Dad? We'll have to stand here a week just to earn three dollars each."

"They won't let you stay here overnight," the man ahead of them said. "We might as well leave. There won't be no more trains today."

"Come on, Roy," Harlow said. "Let's tag along. I could use a cool glass of beer. Then we'll get our things and, come dark, head for the freight yard." He slapped the tall farmer on the back. "Come along, friend. You need a beer, too."

12

In the dark cool barroom, Harlow set Roy and the farmer in a booth. He returned with two foaming schooners of beer and a bottle of Dr Pepper. He touched the rim of his mug to the other schooner and Roy's bottle. He put it to his lips and drank until it was empty. He wiped the froth from his lips.

"That hit the spot. It's time to have another." He went to the bar.

"Some men like whiskey," Harlow confided to the farmer and his son who drank slowly, "and some men, and women, too, I hear, are partial to wine, but I always thought of beer as a man's drink. It feels good going down, and it lets you know when you have had enough. Yes, sir. There's nothing like beer straight out of the barrel. I only drink beer from a bottle or one of those cans they put it in now when I have to. Isn't that right, Roy?"

Roy didn't answer. He stared down at the empty Dr Pepper bottle. Why was Dad using up their money like this? He didn't mind sharing with the stranger, who must have been as dry as he and his father were, but Dad had promised back in the kitchen the night they set out that he was through with beer. "It's about time we got our bags and headed for the freight yard, Dad," he suggested.

The sad-faced farmer spoke for the first time, "You men heading on?"

"That's right," Harlow said loudly. "I can see that there's nothing here for us. The whole town's about ready to blow away in the next dust storm. I have an important job waiting for me in California. Roy here is going back to school. They say a man can live decent out there. You want to come along with us? I can fix you up with a job when we get there."

The man shook his head. "Naw. I got a wife and a little girl to look after. They're at my mother's place, been there since I lost the farm. They won't be wanting to leave. Thank you for the beer. I wish you both good luck." He shook hands with Harlow and Roy.

"That was a fine, soft-spoken man, wasn't he? I think I'll have another one and we'll take off, too. The bartender said they brewed their beer right here in the cellar. That's the best way, I always say. A man in the kitchen at the prison used to make home brew and sell it. It never tasted like much."

By the time they reached Sycamore Street, Harlow was unsteady on his feet and talking silly to Roy, his arm around the boy's shoulder.

"You sit here in the rocker," Roy said. "I'll get our things from inside."

"You do that, Roy," his father said. "I'll stay here on the porch and behave myself. No need to hurry. You heard them say you had to wait until evening." Harlow

55

leaned his head back. His mouth dropped open, and he snored.

"No luck, eh, son?" Mrs. Franklin said. "I thought not. Even if you're at the head of the line, the foreman sometimes jumps over you if he doesn't know you and calls up his friends. I prepared you and your father a bag of sandwiches to take with you. There won't be any dining car hitched on to the cattle train."

"Thank you very much, ma'am. You've been good to Dad and me. We won't forget it."

Mrs. Franklin's eyes watered. "That's what God put us here for, son, to help others along when they need help. Are you going to be all right with your dad? He looks bushed out."

What did she mean? Had she smelled the beer when she opened the front door for Roy? Or maybe she had seen Dad with the rent can in his hands? "We'll be all right," he answered. "Dad hasn't been well for a spell, but he's coming around now. Once we get to California everything will be fine."

The sun was a huge ball of orange-red fire slipping out of sight beyond the fields when Roy and his father came across the stockyards to the train tracks. A powerful black engine was moving back and forth, coupling empty cattle cars to the train.

"We'll stay away from the tracks," Harlow said. "Isn't that what the drugstore man told us, 'Stay out of sight'?"

Roy nodded. He followed his father along a dirt path well back from the tracks. They came to people sitting or hunched down behind the dusty bushes, waiting, like cats for their supper, for the train to pull out. Mostly they were single men in worn clothes, some with a canvas bag or a gunnysack, others with a cloth tied at the four corners. And one woman, a tired-looking young woman with a baby slung over her back in a kind of hammock, was kneeling beside a young man. They were holding hands.

A space separated the couple from a group of black men farther down the path. "I reckon this is a good place, Roy," Harlow said. He squatted, closer to the young couple than to the big black man in striped overalls and a dirty felt hat.

"Do you know what to do, Dad?" Roy asked. "The train will be moving, won't it? They won't be leaving the doors open, I figure."

"It won't be hard," Harlow said. "We just do what the folks down the line are doing. He took a deep breath and blew it out. "Give me one of those sandwiches, Roy. I should have taken a couple of eggs from the bar when I got the beer. I was so thirsty I wasn't paying attention. Beer on an empty stomach makes you a little dizzy."

Dad didn't look well. Roy unwrapped the wax paper from a baloney sandwich and handed it to his father. "I'll go find out what we ought to do."

"Okay, Roy."

The boy walked down the path to the man in striped overalls. "Excuse me," he said. "We figure on catching the freight train when it comes by, only we haven't ever done it before. Can you tell me what to do? My dad isn't feeling good."

The black man looked up at Roy, then to his right toward Harlow and the couple with their baby.

"Looks like half the people in the country is fixing to ride free, if they can." He shook his head. "It ain't hard once you learn how. What you got to do is keep in step with the train—don't fall back—and swing yourself into the car if the door is open. Sometimes they bolt the door shut, so you have to slip the bolt and push it open. It depends. You and your pa watch me, I'll get us a car to ride in. You tell him to be careful not to slip under the wheels. Run alongside until I give you a hand. The engine will be picking up speed right about here. Those folks with the baby, they friends of yours?"

"No," Roy said.

"They got no business traveling with a baby. They don't look like they know what they're doing. You tell them what I said."

"Thank you," Roy said. "Thank you, sir."

The man touched the brim of his hat.

From down the tracks, the call went up, "Here she comes." The people waiting stood up. Roy could hear a hum along the track. "Come on, Dad," he said. "This man will help us. You too," Roy said to the couple. "If you want to."

The people moved forward to the edge of the tracks, ready to run. It was almost dark. The engine approached, gathering speed. The engineer in his striped cap and red bandanna around his neck looked straight ahead. He's telling us it's all right with him, Roy thought.

The big man motioned them to start moving alongside the cars. "Here's one for us," he called. He shoved up the bolt and pushed the slatted door open. He sat on the edge of the car, holding his hand out. He pulled Harlow into the cattle car, then Roy and the young man. The woman with the baby fell a step behind. She could not reach the outstretched hand. The black man jumped to the ground, swept the woman and her baby up and shoved them into her husband's arms. Then he swung himself inside.

"Man," he laughed, "we just about didn't make it. You all know what to do the next time in case I'm not around." He pushed the door shut and slumped to the floor.

13

The cattle car smelled of manure. Harlow and Roy leaned against the wall opposite the door, canvas bags between their legs. The couple tucked themselves in a corner of the car out of the wind. The baby cried softly. The woman shifted the bundle to her breast. Embarrassed, Roy turned his eyes away.

"This isn't up to our standards of travel, is it, Roy?" Harlow said. "Aren't you sorry now we didn't borrow a few dollars from the coffee can? I would have sent it back when we got established in California."

Roy tried not to listen. No matter what Dad said, it was stealing. Maybe it was one thing to burn Frank Cochran's shack down when they left Tilson, because Mr. Cochran had lied to send Dad to jail, but Mrs. Franklin had taken them in and fed them and done their laundry, all for a dollar.

Roy opened the package of sandwiches and held one out for his father. "I can't eat with this smell in my nose," his father said. "I'll wait awhile, son."

Roy stood up. He went to the corner to offer the couple a sandwich. "We got lots of them if you want it." The man took the sandwich without a word. He broke it in two and offered half to his wife. Roy urged them to take another. "What's the baby's name?" he asked.

"Frankie," the woman answered, not lifting her eyes.

The boy turned to the man who had helped them into the car. He appeared to be asleep, head falling forward onto his chest. "Do you want a sandwich?" Roy said. The man looked up and reached out a massive hand for the sandwich. He passed it under his nose and smiled. "It smells good, boy, like there's some meat inside. It's been two days since I ate. I thank you."

"How far will the train go?" Roy asked.

"It ain't how far it will go, it's how far they will let us go. Sooner or later they'll stop and clean the cars of people. There's no telling when. You better get your sleep while you can."

Harlow was already asleep. His breathing made a gurgling sound. From time to time he coughed to clear his throat, but it started right up again. The gurgle had something to do with the drink, Roy was sure. When Dad had flopped out on the bed the Saturday nights he came home full of beer, he used to make the house shake with noises like that. Ruth Ann would sit up all night in the kitchen, her head resting on the table.

Roy wondered if Ruth Ann had made it home to West Virginia. Traveling was expensive, and maybe she'd run out of money, too. If he had known when she was taking off, he would have given her ten dollars from his wallet, so she could have bought Lilian and herself some food along the way and a candy bar or two extra for Lilian. He hoped they were all right.

Things had happened so fast he could scarcely keep up with them. Ruth Ann and Lilian gone, the house by the marsh burned down, a bus trip halfway across the country—or more, according to the ticket agent—and now, riding west in a cattle car, expecting to be thrown off in the middle of nowhere, maybe even in the dark. Whatever happened from now on, Roy determined he was going to keep his father out of saloons. He put his canvas bag under his head and stretched out. He wished he could see the stars and smell the breeze off the bay when the tide was racing in. His thoughts passed into dreams, lulled by the steady clackety-clack of the iron wheels on the rails.

The motion slowed. Roy sat up uneasily. How long had he been asleep? It was still dark; the warm air no longer pushed through the slats. He looked around. Someone was standing beside the door, the black man. He had opened the door a foot or so and was listening. Roy pulled himself up and joined him. "What's going on?" he asked.

"They're pulling onto a siding up ahead. You can feel it in the rails. Get your pa ready. And those folks with the baby."

The couple was asleep, kind of leaning on each other, holding hands again. The baby lay in the nest of his mother's lap. Roy bent over. He touched the young father's shoulder. "Wake up," he whispered. "We may have to jump off in a hurry."

The man started. "What?" he mumbled. He sat up straight.

"You and your wife and baby better get ready," Roy

repeated. "We might have to jump out. I'll help you with the baby."

The train ground to a halt, wheels screeching against the brake plates. A tremor passed from car to car, shaking the people inside. After a moment of silence, shouts and beams of light piercing the darkness at both ends of the cattle train.

"They're hitting the cars with clubs. It's time to go," the big man called.

Harlow climbed to his feet, uncertain. "What's going on, Roy?"

"We have to leave, Dad. You go jump out. I'm going to help the woman with the baby. You take my bag along with yours."

The banging came closer. "Give me the baby," Roy told the woman. "Your man will help you down, then I'll give you Frankie." Roy took the infant tenderly, holding him tight. Frankie felt like Lilian when she was little and he took her on his lap. Even in the stinking cattle car, the baby had a good smell.

"Hurry," the black man hissed. He stood outside the car. He gave a hand to the husband, then his wife. He reached up to take the baby from Roy and gave it to its mother. "Get back off the tracks," he commanded, "into the dark where they can't find you with their lights. Maybe we can get back on later."

Harlow waited for Roy to lead him toward the edge of darkness. Again he asked, "What's going on, Roy?"

"The guards are clearing out the cars. We have to wait here in the dark out of sight to see if we can get back on. Give me the bags, Dad. I'll take them for a while."

There was a cornfield down the grade from the siding. Roy tripped over the stubbles. Harlow waited for him to get up. "This is far enough, son."

"Get down on your knees," the big man advised them. "They'll be shining their lights over here. They can pick you out if you're standing up."

The baby whimpered. "Shh," his mother whispered. She crooned softly to the child.

They waited in the night while the noises faded away and the lights disappeared. Down the tracks, the engine hissed and lurched forward. The cars rattled by, one by one. Deep at the edge of the grading, shadowy figures, bent over, approached the train. Suddenly flashing lights dug into the darkness. Roy heard thuds and sharp cries of pain.

"Those men should have known better. Happens all the time," their guide muttered. "We'll just hunker down here in the field until dawn and find out where we're at. It's a lonely place to be left behind."

"Why did they do that?" Harlow complained. "We weren't hurting anything. Why do they do that to poor people?"

The black man laughed softly. "They own the railroad, mister, that's why. They can do what they want to, they don't care about us."

14

They waited for the first light of day in the stubbled cornfield. Harlow stretched out, his head resting in Roy's lap. The father held his baby over his shoulder, his wife's head in his lap. He stroked her long hair, pushing it off her face. The black man sat apart, humming to himself.

At the first touch of dawn, Roy could see the gray outlines of a small town, divided by the tracks. "Do you know where we're at?" he called to the black man.

"Naw, these towns all look alike. Must be a crossroads. They had the bulls waiting for us. That's what they do, the company, move them up and down the line in trucks. They stop the train and chase us off and break our heads if we try to climb back on, mostly at night so we can't see what we're doing. They got their tricks, right enough."

He stood up and stretched. "Another thing, folks like us aren't welcome in these little places. They got their own problems and they don't want no more. What you learn to do when you ride the rails is walk on down beyond the town. The trains slow up as they come through. They don't stop, just slow up enough so's you can hop aboard if you're quick—and careful. You got to know what you're doing. It ain't nothing for a woman or a sick man like your pa to be doing."

The talk woke Harlow up. He rubbed his eyes. "Where are we at, Roy?"

"I don't know, Dad. Just out in a cornfield somewhere."

"Come along," the black man said. "I'll take you to the road. You all will be better off hitching a ride on the highway. Some trucks will be coming along when it gets light. They might stop if they see the baby, you can't never tell what a driver will do. One thing, though, they sure won't stop for me."

They trudged along the tracks into the small town, which was only a main street with a couple of stores and some weatherbeaten houses lined up on dirt streets along both sides of the railroad tracks. On the far end of town a paved road ran across the tracks east and west.

The big man stopped. He pointed westward to a couple of trees on the horizon. "Keep going till you get to the trees," he told them. "Sit there in the shade and let the boy here catch you a ride."

"What about you?" Roy asked. "Where are you going?"

"Anywhere the train goes. I'll jump the first freight that comes along, it don't matter. Things are bad wherever you go. I'll light down when I find a place that wants me."

"Here," Roy said. He took the last sandwich from his bag. They could buy more in the town. "Good luck."

"You, too, sonny. You're going to have to look after

66

these folks, I can see that. I reckon you're man enough to do it." He took Roy's hand and gave it a shake.

The sun rose higher in the sky. A stifling heat settled on the highway. Roy squatted beside the road. When a car or truck approached headed west, he stood up, held his arm out straight, his thumb pointing. Not many cars or trucks passed, and only one, a Ford roadster, slowed down. When the driver saw the people under the tree, he shook his head at Roy to tell him there wasn't room for them and kept on going.

The father came up to Roy. "We have to get some water for the baby. I'm going into town."

"You got any money?" Roy asked.

"A little. I'll buy us a loaf of bread."

"Wait a minute," Roy told him. "There's a truck headed our way from town. Let's us both stand here and put our hands out."

An old farm truck pulled to a stop. The driver leaned across to shout out the window, "I'm only going down the road a piece. I been to town to get gasoline. Will a couple of miles do you any good?"

That wasn't going to help, Roy thought. He let the young man answer. "Do you have some water there?" the husband asked.

"Sure do. That's about the only thing we have left, a well that works." He saw the baby. "Why, you got a baby with you. It's too hot out here for a baby. Tell your wife to get in front with me. You men can ride in the back."

In a few minutes the truck turned onto a rutted dirt road that passed through a barren field to a dusty farmyard. A barn door was banging back and forth in the hot breezes. An iron cock weathervane on top of the barn spun round and round. The farm looked deserted.

"There's nothing left, is there?" the farmer said. "I sold my stock in the spring. It didn't do any good. Come on inside. Mother will give you some cool water and whatever else we have, which isn't much. Then I'll drive you back to a shady place on the road for you to get to wherever you're going."

Inside the front door, furniture was collected. A wicker trunk and two carpet bags were piled on the marble-topped parlor table. The farmer led them through a dim hallway to the kitchen. "I brought you some guests, Mother," he announced.

He turned to the visitors. "I'm Walt Landon—no relation to the governor—and that's Martha, and the girl sitting at the table is our daughter, Mary. Our boy joined the Army last year, so he isn't home. Sit down at the table. Later on, maybe one of you can help me load it onto the truck, along with the chairs. They need water, Mother, fetch the pitcher."

Mrs. Landon came up from the cellar with a crockery pitcher. She gave the young woman a jelly glass. "What's your baby's name?"

"Frankie, that's what we call him. His proper name is Franklin, like the President's. I'm Emily. My husband is Ted, Ted Wheeler. We're from Ohio."

"Harlow Purdy and my boy, Roy," Harlow spoke up. "We're obliged to you. They threw us off the train last night. We were hoping to get farther west before they did."

"That's what they do all the time to the cars coming out of Wichita. They let the cattle ride in the cars, but not people. That don't seem right to me, but that's what they do. Where you folks headed?"

"Los Angeles, California," Harlow said proudly.

"Anywhere I can find a job," Ted Wheeler said. "The bank took my farm back home. Our folks are gone, so we figured on starting over somewhere else. When our old car broke down for good in Missouri, we started hitching. Our luck ran out in Wichita."

Mr. Landon looked at his wife. "Isn't that something? You came to the right place," he said ironically. "The bank foreclosed on our place, too. Gave us fifteen days to get off the land. This farm has been in our family for eighty years, since when there were Indians here. The bank didn't care. We borrowed the money, they said, and if we couldn't meet the payments, they'd have to take the place over. Now it's theirs, and we'll be moving on, too."

"Where you going?" Roy asked. There didn't seem to be any place you could go where there was work.

"California," Mr. Landon said. "A man came through here last week telling folks there was lots of work out there in the orchards and farms. Land, too, they're selling cheap. Mother and I have a little money set by the bank doesn't know about; enough to get us there. No dust storms in California, they say. Well, Mother, don't you have anything to feed our guests? It don't seem right to send them on their way hungry."

"They're welcome to whatever we have, which isn't much. You cut the bread, Mary, while I bring up some things from the cold cellar."

Mrs. Landon held out her arm to the girl. The girl rose awkwardly to her feet. Roy saw that her left leg was in some sort of metal contraption from her feet up to under her shirt. Two crutches leaned against the table.

Seeing Roy look at her leg, Mary blushed. "Polio," her mother said to Roy. "It's not your fault, Mary. There's no need to feel embarrassed. We thank the Lord every day you didn't have it in your other leg, too."

15

"You take that side of the table, Roy," Mr. Landon said, "and we'll ease it out the kitchen door and around to the truck. If you have time, you could help me with the bed and the bureaus in the front hall. The rest I can manage. I'm real sorry my son isn't here. He'd enjoy the trip west, but he's already halfway around the world."

Where was that? Roy wondered. It was better to keep quiet so Mr. Landon wouldn't figure he hadn't spent much time in school.

The farmer didn't notice his silence. He went on talking about his boy named Matt. "Yes, sir, he is out in the Philippine Islands with the Army. What do you reckon they have him doing out there he couldn't be doing just as well right here in Leavenworth? Okay, Roy, now let's lift it up real careful. We'll put it all the way to the front and pack around it. I'll make a bed for Mary to ride back here. She can't hardly bend her leg with that brace to sit up front. An awful thing to happen to a young girl. In California, maybe they can do something for her. Not cure her so she'll be a ballroom dancer, mind you, but get it to bend a little."

"How old is Mary?" Roy asked.

"Fourteen last April."

"Me, too. I'm fourteen."

"You're mighty big for your age, Roy."

"That's what folks say," Roy answered. "I've been working regular for over a year. If I'd stayed, I'd of been a regular boat builder next year." He shut up. He didn't want Mr. Landon to know what his father did or anything.

Harlow and Ted brought out the kitchen chairs. "Just put them down," Mr. Landon said. "Roy and I will take care of them along with what's left inside."

When the truck was loaded and a mattress stretched out for Mary, Mr. Landon unrolled a canvas over the top and lashed it to either side. "You don't reckon it will blow off, do you, Roy?"

The boy tested the knots. They looked pretty tight. "I don't think so," he replied. "It looks right snug in there. Sort of like a cave." It *was* inviting, better than some narrow bus seats on the Greyhound.

Mrs. Landon was waiting for her husband in the front hall. She stepped aside for Roy to pass through. He could hear her whispering to her husband. "Your father has the truck fixed up real nice for you," Roy said to Mary. "It will be like your own private room, almost."

The girl blushed. "I'm a lot of trouble to Ma now," she said. "I wish I could help more. It seems like their trouble started when I took sick."

"Don't you ever talk that way, Mary," Mrs. Landon said from the doorway. "Don't you ever think that way neither. Your dad would have sold this farm a hundred times over for you to be healthy, and never given it a thought. You're our girl and we have you safe and alive with us—we don't want anything more. Just you remember that, Mary, when you start feeling sorry for us, or for yourself."

To the others, she announced, "Walt has something to say."

"Well," her husband began, turning red under his farmer's tan. "Mother had a thought she wants me to tell you about. I was thinking the same thing while Roy and I were packing up the truck, but I didn't know how to put it properly. It does seem a shame to carry all that empty space in the truck to California when there are folks here with us who could fill it. Mother and I—Mary, too, I can tell from the way she looks at Roy—want to take you, Ted and Emily, and you, Harlow, if you want to come along with us. The only thing is," Mr. Landon paused and turned redder still, "we'd have to ask you to look after your own keep. I never asked before—what we had we always shared—but Mother says we don't have enough to feed you from the money we set aside. That's about it."

Emily hugged her baby and wept. Her husband held her tight. "God bless you, Mr. and Mrs. Landon," he cried. "We were about ready to give up." He reached in the pocket of his pants. He counted the bills in his hand. "It's all we have, twenty-two dollars. Will that be enough?"

When Harlow didn't answer, Roy spoke up. "Dad and I have as much, maybe a dollar more, don't we, Dad, counting my five dollars?"

Harlow flushed. He didn't take the money from his pocket. "That's about right, Roy," he admitted.

"You can spell me at the wheel, Ted, if you have a mind to. The farthest I ever drove was to Wichita. Can you drive, Harlow?"

Harlow shook his head.

"Well, two of us is enough. I'll fill up the water bags and we'll be on our way. There's nothing here to keep us. Let the bank have it. Why don't you settle yourselves in, Emily and the baby with Mother up front. There's lots of room in back for everyone else. Roy, you give Mary a hand up." Mr. Landon went down to the cellar, humming happily.

16

Mary was propped up on the mattress, her long, light brown hair blowing across her face. Roy watched as she kept pushing it in back of her ears. Could she use his hat? he wondered. He took it off and wiped the sweatband with his handkerchief. He offered it to the girl. "Do you want this?" he asked. "A lady in Wichita gave it to me to keep the sun off. It was her husband's, but he didn't use it anymore, she said."

Mary blushed. At home she almost never went outside. She wasn't able to help Ma anymore, and there wasn't much to do in the barnyard except feed the chickens, and they had eaten all of them up. When Pa took her to the end of the road to meet the school bus, they sat in the cab waiting for it to come by.

The brace was still too heavy and uncomfortable to drag around on her crutches. She was ashamed of it. The kids didn't tease her, but they looked at her funny when she stood up, like she was some sort of a strange animal they hadn't seen before. Now she saw Roy's eyes were drawn to the high-topped brown shoes she had to lace up tight every morning—"orthopedic" shoes they called them at the hospital—before Ma put the brace on. She blushed and tried to pull her foot under the hem of her long skirt, but it wouldn't go.

Mary reached out to take the hat. Roy watched as she rolled her hair up and slipped the hat on. It was loose, but it stayed on. "Thank you," she said. "We can take turns."

Roy kept on staring. "Naw, I don't need it. I just took it because Mrs. Franklin offered. You look real pretty in the hat," Roy stammered. Blushing, himself, he went on. "I mean you look real pretty anyway, but you look even prettier in the hat."

Roy turned around to look at the black highway slipping away behind them. If you watched long enough it made you kind of dizzy. He thought about Mary. She *was* pretty. Maybe Lilian would look like that when she grew up. She had the same color hair as Mary. He didn't know how to talk to girls; he had really only talked to one since he left school, Mr. Whitlock's granddaughter who used to come down to the boat shed when her mother went off in the afternoon. Mostly she had talked to Maynard, flirting a little bit, it had looked like to Roy. When she went home, Maynard always said, "Lucy's stuck on you, Roy, but she don't want to show it, so she talks to me to make you jealous."

Mr. Whitlock would laugh. "That's how they catch you, Roy, they get you jealous. Then they trap you. Isn't that so, Maynard?"

"That's how my old lady caught me," Maynard would agree. "Otherwise, I'd still be single going fishing on Sunday. You better watch out, Roy."

He hadn't paid any attention. Maynard had liked to tease him every chance he got. Lucy hadn't paid him any mind at all. She was stuck up. Her father, Mr. Whitlock's son David, was manager of the grain and feed store and had been to college just like Dad—except that David had finished, Mr. Whitlock used to say.

"How long will it take to get to California?" Mary asked.

"I'll ask Dad," Roy replied. He leaned across the truck to where Dad sat, eyes closed. "How long to California, Dad?"

"It shouldn't take more than three days, I figure. Walt said he wouldn't stop any more than he had to, maybe every once in a while to let the truck and the rest of us catch our breath. The bus took four days to get as far as Wichita, counting all the connections. Three days, I'd say, if the truck doesn't break down."

"Three days." Roy repeated it to Mary. "How long has your dad had the truck?"

"He bought it secondhand from Mr. Swinton when the old Ford gave out. It's a Reo, a real good truck. Dad says they don't make them anymore. If it was to break something, he's not sure they can find the parts to fix it."

Roy crossed his fingers and held them out for Mary to see. She was nice as well as pretty. Her mother had said maybe they could do something about her leg out in California. Roy knew about polio. The Murray twins he started in school with had both died of polio last summer, first Paul and a month later, Billy. He had seen Mrs. Murray at the American Store after that; it looked like she wasn't interested in staying alive. And Mr. Broadwater, who owned three draggers, a big strong man, he was in a wheelchair for the rest of his life. Ruth Ann used to say they didn't have any polio in West Virginia and if it got any worse in Tilson she was taking Lilian there, even if Harlow was still in prison.

"Is it heavy to walk with the brace?" he asked Mary.

The girl nodded. "Some days it isn't as heavy as other days. Ma says they are making lighter ones now, but we don't have the money for one yet."

Still curious, Roy asked if it hurt much.

"It used to hurt dreadful, but not so much anymore. After a while, the doctor says, it won't hardly hurt at all. And I'll be able to get around better when I'm stronger. With one crutch, maybe, or none at all. Ma says so, too."

"I sure hope so," Roy said. He crawled across the truck to sit next to Harlow. "Are you all right, Dad?"

"I'm all right, Roy, a little stiff from sitting, maybe, but I'm all right. I was thinking about yesterday. I should have taken a couple of boiled eggs with the beer. That's what did it, an empty stomach."

"You're through with drinking now, aren't you, Dad?"

"It looks that way, doesn't it, Roy? I don't think Walt is going to pull up in front of any saloons along the way. What do you think, Ted?" he asked the young farmer next to him.

"How's that, Mr. Purdy? I didn't hear you."

"Nothing," Harlow said and put his head back against the panel. "Someday, Roy, I'm going to have a car of my own, a big Buick or even a Packard. We'll drive to Tilson all the way across the country in the summer when the school is out. Yes, sir, that's what we'll do. How about that?"

Roy wasn't thinking about the Chesapeake Bay and the boat shed. For some reason, he was worrying about Mary Landon and what she was going to do in California. "I reckon so, Dad," he answered, "if that's what you'd like to do."

17

Walt Landon and Ted Wheeler peered at the smoking engine of the Reo truck. "It's not only the radiator this time," Mr. Landon said. "It's the whole blessed engine. I reckon the poor old Reo didn't know what to do out here on the highway and gave up. It's never been very far from the farm, just like Ma and Mary and me. Still, it don't seem right for it to die right now when we have put those mountains behind us. We're almost to California."

The Reo rested beside the highway, a few yards short of a sign saying it was only forty-five miles to the California line. On either side, rocks and scrub bushes stretched to the horizon. Ahead of them the sun was about to disappear. Roy left Mary and Harlow in the back of the truck; in the cab Mrs. Landon and Emily were taking turns trying to comfort the crying baby.

"I had a tractor that behaved the same way," Ted said. "It didn't want to go in the heat. I had to do my plowing early in the morning or in the last little bit of light in the evening. The John Deere man said old tractors were like human beings, you couldn't push them all the time. Maybe that's what's wrong with your truck, Walt. Did it ever give you any trouble before?"

"When it did, Seth Swinton—he had the farm next to mine—took a look at it and got it running again. Too bad he's not here now. He lost *his* farm last year and took off for Kansas City. He found a job there in the packing plant, I hear. All I know how to do is put gasoline in the tank, change the oil, and put water in the radiator. It's all I've had to do since Seth went away."

"How about the oil?" Ted asked. "You haven't put oil in since we left."

"I changed it the day before. We haven't gone three thousand miles yet."

Ted looked under the hood. He lifted out the dipstick. He ran it between his thumb and forefinger and put it back. He took it out again and looked at it. "It's dry," he said. "The engine might be blown. You carrying extra oil in back?"

Walt shook his head. "I'll hitch me a ride back to the gasoline station we passed. How far would you say it was?"

"Five or six miles."

"I'll go," Roy said.

"You want to do that for us, Roy?" Mr. Landon asked. "Ted or I can go just as well."

"I'll be all right," Roy said.

"Well, if you don't mind, we'd be obliged. Let's see, get us five quarts of oil. And if you could fill one of our water bags, too, we're about out." Walt reached in his pocket for money.

"I got money, sir," Roy said. He took one of the water bags off the front bumper and headed down the road. It felt good to get out of the truck and on the ground. He stretched the muscles in his legs. He could get to the station and back in three hours easy. He might even pick up a ride, though most of the traffic they had seen was going the other way, toward California. Old cars and trucks with scared-looking people inside, farmers most of them, he bet.

Three days without stopping, except at the gasoline station and sometimes in the hills to give the truck a rest when it was about to boil over. Just like on the bus, except that it was a lot more comfortable in the truck and he had someone to talk to. He hoped Mary would think he was pretty brave to be walking to the gasoline station in the dark. He'd have something to tell her when he came back. He and Mary never got tired of talking to each other, explaining how it was where they lived and how they grew up. One time Roy almost let it slip that Dad had been in prison. He'd better remember to steer away from those four years. He'd just say they were so poor he had to go to work, and try not to talk too much about Dad.

Dad wasn't listening, Roy was certain. He sat all day across the truck like he was sick, half leaning back, eyes closed, not moving at all for hours on end. Nighttime he lay on his side, doubled up. When they stopped at the gas station he stumbled out of the truck to use the toilet and climbed back up to his place without a word. He left it to Roy to bring him a sandwich and a soda. If Roy asked if he was all right, Harlow nodded without a word. A couple of times Ted, who was lonesome without his wife and Frankie, tried to start up a conversation, but that didn't work, so Ted tended to his own business.

A gasoline truck rolled past before Roy could put his thumb out. It ground to a stop a hundred yards ahead. The driver shouted back to Roy to catch up if he wanted a ride.

"Was that your truck back there by the milepost?" he asked.

"Mr. Landon doesn't know what's wrong. I'm going to the station for oil and water."

"I see four or five cars and trucks every day that won't go anymore," the driver said. "Driving is different out here in the west. Folks from back east or wherever don't understand that. They push their cars up the mountains and across the desert until they give out. They don't go any farther."

"Like the Reo, I guess," Roy said. "What do folks going to California do then?"

"That's a good question," the driver said. "Sometimes they seem to get them going. I'd swear that the old wrecks they drive have a mind to get to California, just like the folks inside. I can't explain. It must be some kind of trust the cars and the drivers have in each other."

The station lay ahead on the right. The tank truck pulled over to the side. "Good luck, kid," the driver said. "You'll probably get a ride back."

The driver was wrong. Carrying the oil in the burlap bag the owner of the station let him have and the full water bag, Roy's arms grew stiff and began to ache. He shifted the loads from one arm to another and trudged on. When he heard a car approach he turned and waited to see if it would stop. Most of them were full of people and their things. It seemed to Roy the man behind the wheel was afraid that if they stopped, the car might never start again.

It was totally dark when he reached the Reo. He could just about see Dad asleep on his back. Mary smiled and waved. She still had Mrs. Franklin's straw hat on; she only took it off when she settled down for good at night.

On each side of the truck, talking to their wives, were Ted and Walt, each with one foot up on the running board, and leaning on the knee.

"Roy is back," Walt called over to Ted. "We'll need a match to find the place to pour the oil in. Bring the screwdriver from the side pocket."

Ted drove the screwdriver through the lids of the cans. While Walt held a match over the motor, he poured the oil into the motor. Afterward, he filled the radiator to the top. He climbed into the cab and pushed hard on the starter. The motor groaned but refused to catch.

"Shall I keep on going?" Ted spoke to Mr. Landon. "If she keeps turning over we'll wear the battery down. It doesn't sound too strong."

"She'll either start or she won't," Walt answered. "Keep on trying."

Again Ted jammed his foot on the starter again and again. The motor growled, not quite so loud.

Roy remembered that Maynard always had trouble with his old Chevy when he started for home after work. He just kept his foot heavy on the starter until he got it going. Sooner or later, it always started up.

"Maybe if you just keep on pushing and don't let your foot up," he suggested cautiously. "It can't do any harm, can it?"

"Go on, Ted. Give it everything this time. Roy's right, it can't do any harm now."

Ted seized the steering wheel with both hands. He braced himself against the seat and pushed hard on the metal button. The motor growled, sputtered, coughed, hiccuped, and settled down to its familiar roar.

"Hold a match underneath to see if she's leaking oil," Ted said.

Walt looked, then ran his hands over the ground. "It's dry. Take her down the road. I'll climb in back with Roy."

18

Over an hour later, the Reo slowed to a crawl. Mr. Landon, who had been sleeping next to Roy, climbed to his feet. "What do you suppose is wrong now?" he asked no one in particular. "I better have a look." When the truck came to a stop, he eased himself to the ground. Mary and Harlow were asleep. Roy joined Walt beside the cab.

Ahead of them on the highway red taillights twinkled in the darkness. A trooper walked along the line of vehicles toward them. As he came closer they could see him handing the drivers a sheet of paper.

"I'll take that. Is something the matter?" Mr. Landon asked.

"You have to fill this sheet out," the patrolman replied. "Name, address, where you're going to stay in California and for how long, and how much money you have with you."

"That seems kind of personal, don't it?"

The patrolman shrugged. "It's none of my business. I

guess they think too many of you people are coming into the state and they can't provide for you."

"It's a free country, isn't it? We can go where we want to, I always heard."

"I'm only handing out the questions, mister. I guess it's a free country if you can pay for it. Talk to the people at the head of the line."

"That beats all I ever heard," Walt complained to Roy. "The man who came through town back home didn't say anything about this." He handed the paper to Ted who was peering out the window. "Ask Ma to fill this out. Hold a match for her if she can't see. We'll walk alongside, Roy, and stretch our legs."

As they moved forward, they could see trucks and cars turn around in the highway and pull off the road headed toward them. A few kept on coming east down the road slowly, ever so slowly.

"It looks like they're not letting some of them cross over into California up there, Roy. What do you suppose is going on?" Mr. Landon asked.

"Maybe Dad knows. His friend Jack O'Neill lives in Los Angeles. He might have told Dad."

"Don't rouse him up, Roy. We'll find out soon enough."

At the head of the line, just beyond a sign saying WELCOME TO CALIFORNIA, two men sat at a table beside the road. By lantern light they examined the papers the drivers gave them. They appeared to be asking the drivers questions.

"Shoot, they're asking to see our money," Mr. Landon said. "It looks like we have to pay to get into the state. I never heard of such a thing. Has Ma finished, Ted? Let me have that piece of paper."

When it came their turn, Mr. Landon handed the paper to a man at the table. He studied it and looked up. "It says here you don't know where you're going, is that right?"

"We're going to wherever there is work, mister, like everyone else in this line. You tell me where I can find any kind of a job to feed my family and I'll tell you where I'm going."

The man ignored the question. "And you say you have about two hundred dollars? Is that correct?"

"I'm not a liar, mister. My wife isn't, either. She filled that out for you. If we say we have two hundred dollars, we have it."

"Could you show it to me, please?"

"You mean I have to pay to enter one of the states of the union? Is that what you mean? I'm an American citizen, just like my folks before me, and their folks before them. We're not immigrants from one of those European countries. I didn't vote for Mr. Roosevelt, but I still am American."

The man sighed. He listened patiently to Walt Landon. "We have an emergency, Mr. Landon. We can't look after any more people who don't have a dime to their names. We have no place to keep them and no way to feed them. The Growers' Association isn't going to look after you, I'll tell you that."

"Who are they?" Roy dared ask.

"They are the growers, and I don't mind telling you, I am ashamed of them. So is the governor. They go to where you folks come from and say there is work and land in California when there isn't any."

"Did you hear that, Roy? That man lied to me. Look, mister, we're here. We can work. We aren't proud. And we didn't come all this way to beg."

The man sighed again. "I'm certain you didn't. The work is seasonal. Right now it's between seasons. There aren't enough jobs in the fields for everyone. So we have to know you can look after yourself for a while. That is all we have to find out and you can go on about your business. Could you show me your two hundred dollars? I only want to see it."

Mr. Landon took a worn brown wallet from his hip pocket. He spread ten twenty-dollar bills on the table.

"Thank you," the man said. "Let him through," he shouted to a policeman standing in the middle of the road, a red lantern in his hand.

"Where do you say we should go?" Mr. Landon asked, as he tucked the bills in his wallet.

"I heard the Association might have some jobs over toward Riverside. The oranges will be coming on pretty soon."

"Then that's where we'll go. You're not too uppity to pick oranges, are you, Roy?"

"No, sir," Roy said. He swung himself into the back of the truck. Mary had turned on her side. In the dim light, Roy saw that she had put her hand under her cheek.

"What was all the talking about, Roy?" Harlow asked drowsily.

"They were checking folks who wanted to get into California. They wouldn't let you in unless you had some money. They said there weren't enough jobs for all the people who were coming out here."

"Not like us, eh, Roy? Jack has a job waiting for me as soon as I show up. They let Walt in, did they? He said he had some money."

"Two hundred dollars. He put it on the table for them to take a look at. That made them pay attention, you can bet."

"That's good to know," Harlow said. "We can save what we have left for when we get to Los Angeles. Did you get your money back for the oil? I saw that Walt didn't give you a dollar to pay for it before you took off."

"It was fifty cents, Dad, ten cents a can at the gasoline station. They didn't charge for the water the way some of these stations we stopped at did. We have to help, too. Ted paid for the last gasoline they put in the Reo."

"What Ted does is his business. Our business is to get where we are going. These farmers started out with something. We started out with almost nothing. You remember that, Roy. We didn't have a farm to sell."

"The bank took their farm, you heard them say," Roy whispered. Walt was climbing into the truck.

"Maybe—and maybe not," Harlow said. "You just be careful with the money you have left, or I'll have to look after it for you."

19

Sometime in the middle of the night, the Reo began to sputter. It lurched forward, slowed, lurched, chugged for a while, and stopped. Roy could hear Ted try to start it, but there was no response. Walt Landon sat up too, a blanket wrapped around his shoulders. "More trouble, I reckon," he said to Roy as they slid off the back of the truck.

"She doesn't want to go any farther," Ted whispered. "Listen." He pushed the starter in vain.

"Well, she's come a long ways," Walt said calmly. "We oughtn't to complain. We'll give her some rest. How far to Riverside?"

"The sign says six miles."

"Where do you suppose we're at?"

"Just outside a place called Cordelia," Ted answered. "Sure is a pretty night. Look at the moon up there. It's like a silver Christmas tree ball."

"We can't do anything until daytime, anyway," Walt said. He walked across the road to a cluster of trees. "Why, these must be oranges. Take a look, Roy."

The boy pulled an orange from a branch hanging low and put it to his nose. It smelled like an orange, but in the dim light of the moon he could see that it was green. "It looks like it's green to me," he said.

Mr. Landon agreed. "I do believe I heard once they come off the tree more green than orange. They put some sort of coloring on them to make them look like oranges. That don't make sense. How did they know an orange was supposed to be orange if it was green?"

"It beats me," Ted said. "We'll find out when we start picking them. It doesn't look like such hard work to me. It must be easier than picking cherries. How much do you reckon they pay you?"

"Like you said, we'll find out when we start picking. Anything is better than plowing a dusty field. Go on, Roy, you and Ted get some sleep. I'll sit up in front."

At sunrise, the Reo turned over without a complaint. Walt drove down the road into Cordelia, a small town with a main street and side streets of neat little white bungalows lined up underneath the palm trees. Mary and Roy stood up in the truck. "It's like a picture postcard," Mary said.

"It's pretty all right," Roy agreed. "I'm glad I came now. Take a look, Dad. I bet this is what Los Angeles is like, only bigger."

Harlow rubbed his eyes and peered between the boards. "I could use some breakfast," he said. "It seems like we haven't had a proper meal since we left."

"Walt said we ought to stop here to get our bearings," Ted told him. "The old truck isn't going to go much farther."

Walt parked the Reo in front of a white stucco building calling itself the Cordelia Café. An OPEN sign was tucked inside the screen door. He came to the back of the truck to help Mary to the street. "I told Mother we ought to celebrate once we came to town. We'd like to invite you all to have breakfast with us."

The waitress led them to a big table in the corner. She bent over Frankie who was reaching and grabbing his feet in Emily's arms. "I got one about his age," she confided. "Where you folks from?"

"Kansas," Emily said. "My husband and I are from Ohio, but we started off in the truck back in Kansas with the Landons."

"That's pretty close to home, Kansas is. We came out from Oklahoma. You ever heard of Tonkawa?"

Emily shook her head. "Maybe Mrs. Landon has."

"Well, I'll take your orders now. What will you be having?"

Walt finished his eggs and sausage, and pushed his chair back. He handed the waitress a twenty-dollar bill. "This will cover it, won't it?" When the waitress brought the change, he asked her, "Maybe you could tell us where we can find a place to stay and where we men can find some work to do."

"There ain't any real place to stay around here. Did you bring a tent? Most folks live in tents or in their trucks. The Association has places where you can pitch a tent, campsites with toilets and a water pipe."

Mr. Landon looked around the table. "We don't have a tent and we've been living in the Reo long enough, it seems to me."

"You might talk to the state agency. They have an office down the street to help folks. Talk to Kevin Olsen.

He's real nice. He managed to find us a place in Riverside a while back. It ain't much, but a lot better than a tent, I can tell you."

"What about work?" Ted spoke up.

"There's no work around here except picking. I expect you know that already. You have to deal with the Growers' Association. They control all the jobs for the farms and orchards." The waitress paused. "I might as well tell you before you find out for yourself. They treat you like dirt. You feel like a slave after a while. My husband couldn't take it, begging for a job just to cut lettuce or pick oranges for almost nothing. He was too proud. Kevin found him a job at the cannery in Riverside. And I got me this job here. Ma looks after the baby, so we scrape by. It's better than what most folks have. You'll see."

"It looks like Kevin is the man we need to talk to," Walt said. He gave the waitress a fifty-cent piece. "I wish it was more, but we're kind of stretched."

"You keep it, sir," she said. "You're going to need it unless you're richer than you look like. Could I hold the baby for a minute?" she asked Emily. "I don't get to hold my own much."

"Does the bus go through here to Los Angeles?" Harlow asked.

"Sure does. It comes from Riverside. It stops on the corner across the street. There's one comes by about every two hours."

On the sidewalk Walt announced he was walking down the street to talk to Kevin Olsen. "You want to come, too, Harlow, and you, Ted?"

The two men declined. "Well, I'll do what I can for us," Walt said. "Are you coming, Roy?"

Roy looked at Mary. She smiled. "Go on with Pa, Roy. I'll stand out here by the truck and take in the sights. It's a whole lot different from the farm."

Kevin Olsen was a tall, thin man with a tired and troubled look. "Millie sent you, did she? She and her husband are about the only people we've really been able to do much for. Everybody that stops at the café for a cup of coffee she sends to us. She calls me the answer man. Twice a week I go on the radio for fifteen minutes to tell anyone who is listening where there are jobs and places to live and where you get medical help. Most folks don't have radios, so I don't think it does much good. What can I do for you?"

"Same as the others, Mr. Olsen. There was a man came through town back home in Kansas saying they had jobs and land out here."

"That was the Growers' Association's man. He shouldn't be doing that, but we can't stop them. Sure, there are jobs. Trouble is there are about five men for every job except in high season. And there's land, just enough to put a tent on. The more men there are, the less the Association has to pay you. It's practically nothing, anyway. There's trouble building up here in the valley. You can feel it. Mister, if you have a place to go home to, I advise you to go back home."

"The bank has my home," Walt said. "We're not proud. Ted—he's in the truck with his wife—and I will do anything to get started. I don't know about you, Roy. You'll be taking off for Los Angeles, I guess."

"They are about to start picking in the orange groves," Kevin said. "They'll send trucks around to the campsites to collect the men, some of them at least. That's all I can tell you. The pay is poor."

"Whatever it is, we'll take it to tide us over," Walt said. "Where can we stay?"

Kevin shuffled through the litter of papers on his desk. "Do you have any money, Mr. Landon—is that what you said your name was?"

"Some, not much."

"They've just opened up the state fairgrounds outside of town for people to use. They can put their tents and trucks there. My office controls that, not the Association. They are letting out some of the buildings, too. They aren't much, but they give you a floor and a roof over your head. But you have to pay three months' rent in advance. I have a place with two rooms. It's ten dollars a month."

"We'll take it," said Walt. "I have a daughter who isn't too well."

"It's better than a tent when it rains, that's about all you can say for the cabins. Give this paper to Hank. He's our man out there. You'll see the fairgrounds on the other side of town. Good luck. Hank will tell you about jobs."

20

Hank pointed to a row of whitewashed wooden buildings. "Except for when we had the state fair, they weren't meant to be lived in."

The cabins didn't look any worse to Roy than the shack on the edge of the marsh where he grew up. "Who stayed here?" he asked Hank.

"Oh, the people who ran the midway, a few farmers and livestock people who were here the whole time. They're dry inside, that's one good thing, and there's a padlock on every door. I'll give you two keys."

"They didn't leave any cots behind, did they?" Ted asked. "We had to sell our furniture, save what we roped on top of the car. When it broke down, we had to leave it with the car."

"We have a few old ones in the loft at the cattle barn. I'll bring a couple for you. Anybody else want one?"

Harlow shook his head. "My boy and I will be moving out in a day or two, as soon as I start my new job."

"The free cabins are close to the latrine," Hank said. "There are showers and basins in them. Not hot water,

97

though. And farther down is the cookhouse. It's got some ranges and tables in it. The firewood is free, courtesy of the state of California. You'll have to share with everyone else."

"Where do the trucks come to load the men to do the picking?" Walt asked. "Ted and I want to start right away. Our money has about given out."

"The lineup is out by the front gate. You'll see. The Association has a bulletin board. In the evening they put up a sign saying how many men they need the next day. Did Kevin tell you they don't take everybody?"

"He told my husband," Martha Landon spoke up. "Do they take women, too?"

"Sometimes, ma'am, but only in the fields, and only at the height of the season. But not to pick fruit. I don't know why; that's the way it is. Anyway, it's getting worse." Hank waved his hand across the fairgrounds. "Look at all those tents and vehicles with more coming in every day. By the end of the week, we'll have to close the gate. This is no fit way for people to live. You wait while I go get you some cots."

"It's still early," Harlow said to Roy. "I'll head into Los Angeles to find Jack. Give me the rest of your money, son. I'll be needing it, most likely."

"Don't you think we should get the truck unloaded, Dad? You can go tomorrow just as easy."

Harlow ran his tongue around his lips. "There's no point in waiting to start. I got you here, just like I promised I would, maybe not in high style, but here we are in California, almost three thousand miles from where we started. School will be opening up soon. We have to get ourselves settled in."

Roy took the last four dollars from his wallet. He didn't give his father the change in the little pocket, about eighty cents as he remembered.

"I'll change my shirt and shave and be on my way. Maybe I won't be back this evening if Jack wants me to spend the night. So don't wait up for me." Harlow took his bag and headed for the latrine.

The men and Roy unloaded the Reo. Mrs. Landon took the broom she had put in the truck before they left and swept the inside of the cabin. Emily sat in the shade of a tall eucalyptus tree and fed Franklin.

"It's not the cleanest place I've ever seen. Well, beggars can't be choosers, can they?" Martha said cheerfully. "Which room do you think the women should have, Emily? The inside one so the men can get up early to go to work?"

"It doesn't matter to me," Emily said.

"We'll put the women inside, Pa," Mrs. Landon said, "and leave the men in the room with the door."

Disappointment spread across Ted's face. He opened his mouth to speak, thought better of it, and went on with the unloading. Shoot, Roy thought, Dad and I aren't going to be here long, just a day or two, we can sleep in the truck the time we're here. "It's none of my business," he told Walt, "but Dad and I can use the Reo. We'll pay our share just the same. We'll have the truck for ourselves and you can put the two families together if you want to."

Mr. Landon considered what Roy had said. "That makes horse sense, don't it, Mother? How about you, Ted?"

Ted smiled at Roy. "If it's all right with the others, Emily and I don't want to make trouble."

"That's what we'll do then. We'll put some bedding in the truck. Take the other side of the bureau, Roy. Don't you and Harlow go worrying about paying for sleeping in the truck. Ted and I will arrange the accounts later."

When the truck was unloaded, Roy asked Mary if she wanted to see what the fairgrounds looked like.

"Is it all right, Ma?" she asked her mother.

"You know what the doctor said, Mary. You can do what you want to until you start to hurt. Roy will help you back if the brace acts up."

Roy and Mary made their way along the road that ran around the grounds. The open spaces between the buildings were filled with tents and cars and trucks. Women bent over galvanized washtubs scrubbing clothes. They were hanging the clothes on lines stretched from truck to truck or over the wooden fence along the racetrack. Men in overalls and straw hats squatted in groups of three or four talking softly and picking blades of grass to chew. Children, big and small, many of them barefoot in tattered clothes, played tag or cowboys and Indians.

"I don't reckon they have a school here," Mary said.

"It's still vacation time, Dad said. I've lost track of the time."

"It's about the end of August. I'm not certain of the day or date."

Roy realized that his birthday had slipped by. He had lost track of it in the days after they left Tilson. Every year, no matter what, Ruth Ann had made a cake and bought him a little present—last year a compass he carried in his pocket. They had sung "Happy Birthday" and let Lilian blow out the single candle. For supper they'd had hamburger on buns, not bread, and Roy had had a big dill pickle from the brine barrel in the American Store. He wasn't sure Dad knew any longer when his birthday was; he hadn't said anything this year.

Mary came to the grandstand on the other side of the track. "Could we sit here?" Mary asked. "I'm beginning to hurt a little."

They sat on the plank seat and stared at the fairgrounds. "When do you think the fair comes?" he asked Mary.

"Pa said the man in town, Kevin, told him there won't be a fair. They use the place for folks who have nowhere to go. Have you ever been to a state fair, Roy?"

"Naw. There was one over in Salisbury. We never went. We didn't have a car. We didn't have much of anything, not a proper house like yours, only a shack, no better than the cabin you all are staying in."

"Your dad will do better out here," Mary assured him. "So will we once we have a chance. Ma says things are never as bad as they seem."

"I hope not," Roy said, "but what about all the other folks here and the rest of them that Kevin said were at the campsites?"

"Mr. Roosevelt is going to do something. He's the only one who can, my teacher said. He's the president, you know."

"I heard," Roy said. "You don't have to go to school to know who the president is."

For a second Mary put her hand on Roy's arm. "I'm sorry. I didn't mean any harm."

"It's okay," Roy said. "I learned a lot from Mr. Whitlock and Maynard at the boat shed."

"And your pa, too. I heard him say he went to college. He must have taught you a lot."

"Dad wasn't around sometimes," Roy said. "Wouldn't it be something, Mary, if we were to come back next year when they had the fair going on? We could sit right here in the stands where we are now and watch the sulky races. Wouldn't that be something?"

21

At dawn Walt reached into the back of the truck and shook the sleeping boy's foot. "Come along, Roy," he said. "We're going to the gate. No sense in being the last ones in line when they choose who goes off with them."

Roy sat up and looked around. Dad hadn't come home. Maybe that meant Mr. O'Neill had taken him on right away, and Dad had stayed in Los Angeles to find a place for them to stay. He pulled on his boots and headed for the latrine. The rays of the sun were poking over the mountains to the east. He splashed water in his face and raced to join Walt and Ted at the pick-up place.

"Here's your breakfast, Roy," Walt said, handing Roy a cheese sandwich. "It's all Mother had."

The line of men was longer than the one at the cattle yards in Wichita. Roy didn't hear much talking. Some of the men in nothing more than torn shirts were swinging their arms to keep warm. Until the sun rose the valley was chill.

"The notice says they're taking twenty-five men to-day," Ted remarked. "There's more than twice that ahead of us already. What time do you have to get here?" he asked the man ahead of him.

"That doesn't matter much," was the reply. "They don't take the first men in line necessarily. The foreman goes down the whole line and picks out the ones he wants. I guess the men who get here first think they have a better chance if they're up front."

"How does he know who to pick?" Ted asked.

"Nobody knows. Even if he picked you yesterday, he might not take you today. It's part of their game so they'll always have folks waiting here."

"What do you mean?" Walt inquired.

"The Association wants to keep a lot of people around just in case it needs them all at once. They don't care about the days in between; they don't want regulars. They're afraid of a strike."

"What's a strike?" Roy whispered to Ted. He didn't want the man ahead of them to think he was ignorant.

"It's when people stop working for the company be-cause they don't get paid enough. They stop working un-til they get a promise of better pay or shorter hours or benefits or something. But if you have a whole lot of people who need to work to stay alive, then it's like the man says, a strike isn't going to work. Someone else will take your place."

"That's right, son," the man said. "You can't organize part-time workers. But I hear they are going to try."

A large truck drove through the gate. Two men in brown felt hats and white shirts got out and surveyed the line of men. One of them had a policeman's club in his belt. Roy thought that he looked mean enough to use it.

"That's the security guy," the man in front of Ted said. "Sometimes there's trouble in the line among the men who are passed over. They have wives and children who are going hungry. They're ready to fight. I've seen that fellow knock some heads."

"That's an awful thing," Walt said. "I never heard of beating up people because they need to work. Makes you wonder what's going on in this country."

The foreman came down the line. He touched the men he wanted on the shoulder. "You," he said. "And you." He stopped for a moment to take a look at Roy. "How old are you, boy?"

Roy remembered that his birthday was sometime last week and almost blurted out that he was fifteen. "Me?" he said. "I'm seventeen."

The foreman paid him no more attention. He tapped Ted and passed to the end of the line. The security guard followed, counting the men as they were chosen. "Twenty-five, that's it, Mr. Sykes."

The men selected climbed into the truck and waited patiently. "I'm sorry," Ted said to Walt and Roy as he joined them.

"Come back tomorrow," Sykes called to those left behind. "We'll be taking more of you."

"It looks like we're out of luck, Roy," Mr. Landon said. "We can find something to do around the cabin to keep out of trouble. I noticed the foreman didn't take any two men in a row. Tomorrow you and Ted and

105

I will separate—unless you go off to the city with your dad.''

Hank met them on the road back to the cabins. "No luck, eh?" he said. "I heard the oranges are turning ripe fast. They'll be taking more men from now on. 'Course that means they pay less.''

Hank went on to explain. "It's the kind of game the Association plays with you all. First they keep you waiting until you have nothing left and you'll take any kind of a job. Then they come along and say they can take you but they want to be fair and there's so many men waiting they can't take you all, but if they cut the pay to two cents a bushel instead of three, they can take a lot more of you. That way they get through the season without losing the oranges and without paying any more for the job. You can work all day without filling more than fifty to sixty bushels. You have to carry them to the checker and wait in line to get checked off. As you pick, you discover you work yourself farther and farther away. And you have to climb higher into the trees to get the fruit. They know all the tricks, the Association does. They don't even let you take an orange home to the kids.''

"Maybe we came to the wrong place, Roy," Walt said. "I should have looked to get a job in a plant somewhere. But farm work is in my blood, even if it's only picking beans. We'll have to ask the good Lord to take care of us for a while if we can't do it for ourselves.''

The rest of the morning, Walt helped Martha and Emily scrub the floor and walls of the cabin. Roy washed the back of the truck and played with Frankie for a while. He was beginning to feel restless already. He had been cooped up so long, he couldn't relax. Had Mr. Whitlock and Maynard finished the boat they were working on when he took off? The three of them always had a little celebration when a boat was finished, beer for the men and a bottle of soda for Roy. And they took the rest of the day off, even if they had finished in the middle of the morning. Mr. Whitlock was a good man to work for.

Toward noon, Roy saw Dad coming slowly down the road. His head was down and he seemed to Roy unsteady on his feet. Dad had been drinking again. He hastened to meet him.

"How are you, Roy?" Harlow greeted him. He looked as though he had spent the night in a ditch. His shoestrings were flapping on the ground, and his trousers were stained. He had thrown up on his shirt.

Roy felt embarrassed for his father. He took his father's jacket. "Sit down here in the shade, Dad. Have you been sick again?"

"I believe I have. I haven't eaten much and I feel sort of weak in the head like back in Wichita."

"What happened, Dad? You had enough money to buy yourself some food. You spent it in a saloon, didn't you?"

"They call them bars out here," Harlow said. "This California beer doesn't measure up to National Bohemian. It doesn't agree with my stomach."

"It's the drinking that doesn't agree with you, Dad. You know that by now. You said you were going to stop. Why do you keep on?"

107

"It wasn't my fault, Roy. I found Jack O'Neill, but he was busy and I had to wait until he got off work. He took me across the street to talk about the job. We drank a couple of bottles and Jack went on home. I must have stayed too long. I got lonely, you see, Roy, because you weren't there with me, and I must have gone to sleep somewhere on my way to the bus—in an alley, I guess. They robbed my pockets, somebody did. They missed my ticket or they would have taken that too."

Harlow looked at Roy with bloodshot eyes. "I'm going to stop, Roy. I mean it this time. The woman on the bus I was sitting next to, she got up and moved. I could smell myself. It was awful. I'm done celebrating getting out of prison, I said to myself. Soon as my job starts, Roy and I are starting over."

"You got a job?" Roy asked excitedly.

"I did. I mean I will have one soon, maybe next week. Jack's brother-in-law has this big job with the growers. They're expecting trouble in the valley. Close to here, in Riverside, they're opening an office. Isn't that great?"

"Doing what, Dad?" Roy had a feeling that his father's job was something he didn't want to hear about.

"Security work, like I said. Looking after the fields and orchards, seeing that the pickers don't cause any trouble or tear up the property."

Roy thought of the tough-looking man in the work truck, Mr. Sykes and the man with the black club. "You'll be working for the Growers' Association, won't you, Dad?"

"Sort of, I guess. I don't understand exactly who I'll be working for. It's good pay, son, and it's regular. We'll find a place in town and a school for you to go to."

Roy didn't want to hear any more. "Come on, Dad," he said. "Change your clothes in the truck. I'll borrow some soap and wash your shirt and pants."

22

Roy and his father sat in the back of the Reo, legs over the edge, watching the activity around them. Women came from the cookhouse, most of them carrying a single pot of soup or stew. The children had quieted down to wait patiently for their mothers to spoon out their supper. Whatever was left over, the women took for themselves directly from the pots. The smell of woodsmoke rising from the cookhouse brought to Roy's mind the smell from the range when Ruth Ann set the fire for the evening meal. It was a good smell. Roy heard his stomach gurgle; he was hungry for the taste of warm food.

Harlow took another bite of the baloney sandwich. He made a face and washed it down with a long drink of water from a tin can. "I can't eat any more of this," he said. "Do you want it?"

Roy shook his head. "Here, give it to me. I'll put it in the bread wrapper with the bread and baloney. It's all we have, Dad. I only have twenty cents left. We better hope one of us gets picked out of the line tomorrow."

There was no point in telling Dad he turned down

Emily's offer of a dollar when she and Roy walked to the store in Cordelia, leaving Martha to look after Frankie. He calculated the Wheelers didn't have more than five dollars left. When Dad went to work, he'd see that he paid Ted back something every week for what he spent on them on the ride to California.

He heard Dad say something to him, something to the effect that Roy shouldn't be picking oranges.

"What did you say, Dad?"

"I was just saying it didn't seem right that you and I should be picking fruit, seeing as how I'll soon be working for the Association."

"I don't understand, Dad. What difference does that make? We're broke, like almost everyone else. It's like when you were working for Frank Cochran in the plant. You had to do it for the rest of us. It wasn't any time to be proud."

"That's so, but when I was doing my time, I swore I'd never take that kind of work again, even if I had to end up a bank robber like that Dillinger fellow."

Roy didn't answer. Something was wrong with Dad. He had lost something in the Milford penitentiary.

"Look at it this way, Roy. Jack's giving me a job to protect the people who own the farms and orchards. That sort of makes me like them. We're not pickers, Roy. It just wouldn't look right, the way I see it, for us to do that kind of work. Jack says there is going to be a fight, a strike, he says. We'll be on the other side when it comes."

"Dad, maybe you won't get that job. We don't have any money left, since you were robbed last night." Roy didn't add that some of the money was his.

111

"Walt has a lot. We'll borrow some from him to see us through. I'll pay him back, you can count on it. We'll keep track of just how much it is. Walt won't ever have to ask. We'll drive out here on paydays and give him back the loan."

"I don't think I want to do that, Dad. The two of us can work right now. We don't have anyone else but us. They have the women and Mary and Frankie to look after."

"That's not our problem, Roy. I learned in prison you have to look after number one. That's us."

Roy folded the bread wrapper tight so the bread and the baloney wouldn't dry out. He spread out the old blankets Martha Landon had lent them. "I'm going over to the grandstand. Do you want to come along?"

"You go ahead, son. I'll stretch out here. I'm all worn out. See if my shirt and pants are dry, will you?"

The clothes that Roy had washed and spread over the hood were warm and dry. He folded them and handed them to his father. "I'll be back in a while," he said. "I'll see if Mary wants to go."

"Can we come, too?" Emily asked. "Frankie is cutting a tooth, and it makes him cranky. A walk might do him good."

Ted carried the baby, Emily close to his side. She put her arm around him and hugged him. What would Mary do if I was to hug her like that? Roy asked himself. He turned red at the thought.

"Are you going to the lineup tomorrow?" Ted asked. "It's hard work, I can tell you."

"I'm planning on it," Roy answered. "Dad's job won't start until next week. How much do they pay?"

"Three cents a basket. Not enough, that's for sure. I came home with a dollar and forty cents. You have to pay for the truck ride, too, a dime each way. The Association gets you coming and going." Ted laughed bitterly at his joke.

The grandstand was a quarter filled. After supper most people strolled to the stands and sat there until it was dark. Some of the bigger children ducked under the railing and ran around the track.

Mary took Roy's arm. "Look at the swallows, Roy." She pointed up to the birds darting across the sky for insects.

"The stars are coming out, too," Roy said. He told her about evenings on the Chesapeake Bay, the breezes off the tide as it swept in from the ocean. "I bet you they are the same stars I used to look at back home."

Frankie whimpered. "I'll take him, Emily," Mary said. "You can hold hands with Ted if you want to." She put Frankie on her lap and ran a finger around the baby's gums. When she found the new tooth, she rubbed it. Frankie settled down to chew on her finger. "Look, Roy, he's latched on to my finger. He's sort of cute, isn't he?"

Darkness had settled over the fairgrounds by the time they reached the cabin. Roy could hear Harlow snoring. He unfolded the extra blanket and spread it over his father. He put on his jacket and leaned back against the side panel.

It wasn't fair for Dad not to help out. Walt and Ted weren't watching out for number one. They were doing the best they could for everybody. If Dad wanted to stay out of the lineup, that was his business. Maybe he was right to think he was on the other side. But that didn't mean he could speak for Roy. While Dad was serving time Roy had gone out and found a job for himself. If he did it once, he could do it again.

Drowsy, he stretched out on the floor of the truck. By now the sky was filled with great clusters of stars. A full moon hung low behind the trees. He remembered with pleasure how he had sat close to Mary in the grandstand. When she put her hand on his arm to call his attention to the swallows, she had let it stay there for a minute. He could tell from the smell of soap that Mary had washed her hair. She was a lot prettier than Mr. Whitlock's stuck-up granddaughter Lucy. And a lot nicer. Roy wondered when her birthday was. She hadn't said. If he got to be a regular picker, or whatever he could find to do, he'd buy Mary something special for her birthday. He'd ask her mother when it was when he had a chance. She'd keep a secret. Roy closed his eyes and drifted into sleep.

23

Roy was standing by the Reo before Walt and Ted came out of the cabin. He waited, chewing on a baloney sandwich, until they appeared. Walt nodded; Ted smiled. Both men were a lot more serious than they had been yesterday when they'd marched off to the pick-up, expecting to go to work. They had begun to look like the rest of the sad-faced men in the camp.

They kept in step, not saying anything. It didn't seem to matter to them that Dad wasn't coming along. They took different places in the line. Most of the men were staring at the ground. Some of them had been left behind along with Walt and Roy the day before; they looked like they expected today to be the same.

Two men accompanied Mr. Sykes, the man with the club from yesterday, and another man in a white shirt and black trousers. He pushed his hat back and leaned against the front fender of the truck. On the other side of his belt was a holster. "What's that fellow wearing a pistol for?" Roy heard Ted ask. No one answered.

Sykes and his guard came down the line. He shook

Roy briefly by the shoulder. "Okay, kid. We'll give you a try."

Walt joined Roy in the truck. "It looks like you and me today," he said. "They passed over Ted and most of the men they took yesterday. It beats all how Sykes can remember who to pick and who to leave behind."

"Oh, he remembers all right," the man next to them said. "If he hears you grumble or you don't walk straight or whatever, you'll spend the next week right here waiting. He's mean."

The truck deposited the men at the edge of the orange grove. "Go get your bag from the checker," the foreman Sykes instructed. "He'll take ten cents out of your pay. Be careful with the bag. If you bust it, you'll have to pay for it."

The checker gave Roy a canvas bag to slip over his shoulder. "Ted forgot to tell us about the bag," Walt muttered. "Counting the ride here and back, we're thirty cents behind before we even start. We better get busy, Roy. We'll follow the other men to learn what to do."

The man ahead of them moved quickly among the trees until he came to a section of trees thick with oranges. He went to the end of the row for a bushel basket. "Your first time?" he asked Roy and Walt.

"Yeah," Walt said.

"First, be sure you don't pick green fruit. If they see any green ones, they won't pay you for the basket, even if it's only one orange. You can start here. The trees in back of us are picked out for a while." The man reached up to pluck an orange that was hanging low. "Take the ones like this. You'll find a picking ladder at the end of the row. Don't break the branches. They don't like that either; they might run you off if they was to see you busting a big branch. When your basket is full, take it to the checker. Okay, you're on your own."

Roy set to work. It was a lot different, he soon discovered, from the night they had to stop outside Cordelia. All you had to do there, it appeared, was reach up to take an orange off the tree. You didn't have a canvas sack biting into your shoulder getting heavier with every orange you dropped into it. Two bags filled the basket. It was a heavy load to carry to the checker, the bag flapping behind to trip you if you weren't careful. Already a line of men were waiting ahead of him. The checker wasn't in any hurry. He picked through the basket to see if every orange was ripe. Once in a while he shook his head for the picker to put the basket to one side. When Roy came to the table, the man took his name and put a check on the line beside it. "Make the next one full, kid," he warned.

The sun rose higher. In the trees the air was still. Stinging insects—wasps, hornets, yellow jackets—swarmed over the rotting fruit on the ground. Even when they were stung, the pickers didn't stop for a second. Like ants they carried their baskets to the checker and ran back to the trees, pausing only to swallow a dipperful of warm water from the barrel at the end of the checker's table.

"I didn't bring us no lunch," Walt said to Roy when they met at the end of the row. "Mother didn't have much to give us, and Ted said we wouldn't have time to eat. Can you make it through until supper?"

"I'll make it," Roy said finally. "I got to make it. Dad and I don't have any money."

117

Walt studied him for a minute. He slapped him on the back. "You're a good boy, Roy. But you stay close to me just in case."

Later in the afternoon, Sykes came through the orchard telling the men to fill their baskets and collect their pay; it was time to break off for the day.

Sykes and the two security men stood at the table while the checker read off the names of the pickers. As he handed their wages to them, Sykes told them to move to one side. One of the pickers, a big middle-aged man in striped overalls, didn't move. He spread the change out in the palm of his hand to count it coin by coin. "What are you paying today?" he demanded.

"Two and a half cents," Sykes replied. "Move on out of the way."

"They say it was three yesterday."

"Maybe it was and maybe it wasn't. It's two and a half today. Keep on moving."

The man didn't move. "Why didn't you tell us when you picked us up?"

The foreman looked steadily at the man. "Would it have made any difference?" He looked at the list. "You're Wilder, are you?"

"Yes, Tobias Wilder."

"Well, Mr. Wilder," Sykes said sarcastically, "you came to pick and you have been paid for what you did. Since you don't like what you were paid, you stay in bed tomorrow. Tell your old lady you don't feel like working. Next man, move up."

"It ain't right," Wilder said shuffling to one side. "Folks can't live on what you pay."

"Nobody made you come to California, Wilder. Nobody's keeping you here. Get on back to Iowa or wherever you're from."

Wilder walked to the truck. "It ain't right. It just ain't right."

"Purdy!" the foreman called. Roy moved up to the table. The checker handed him three quarters, a dime, and three pennies. Eighty-eight cents, Roy counted; that was only twenty cents more than he paid yesterday for two loaves of bread and some cold cuts. He held the money out to Walt who climbed in the truck after him. "It isn't much, but you take it."

"I can't do that, Roy," Walt said.

"You have to," the boy said. "Dad says he has a job starting next week. I can't give you any more now. He says he had to spend all we had in Los Angeles. But we mean to pay you back for everything you have done for us. It's no more than right."

Walt took the money. "Thank you, Roy. We appreciate it."

Harlow was sitting by the road waiting for his son. He had on his clean shirt and trousers. "Evening, Walt," he said. And to Roy when Mr. Landon had walked on toward the cabin, "What do you mean going off while I was asleep?"

"Were you going with us, Dad?" Roy asked wearily.

"There was no call for you to go. I'm waiting here for Jack—or whoever he sends—to put me on the payroll."

His son shook his head in despair. "While you're waiting, I'm going to pick, if they'll take me. We owe Walt and Ted for what they've done, and I'm bound to pay them. Don't you try to stop me."

The words echoed in his head as he walked away.

119

They didn't sound like something he would say. He hoped Dad wouldn't think he was mad with him. As he passed the cabin, he saw Ted and Walt in conversation with a stranger. He wasn't one of the men from the campground, he was sure. He was dressed different, and he didn't look like a man out of work.

"Hold on a minute there, Roy," Walt said. "You might as well listen. You're one of us long as you're here. This is Peter Barlow. He wants to help us."

"That's not quite right," the stranger said with a smile. "I'm telling you how you might help yourselves."

"He's what they call a labor organizer," Ted explained. "Kevin Olsen sent him around."

"Don't say that. I don't work for the state. Kevin said it was all right if I came to talk to you people. He didn't send me. You're all tired out, aren't you, Roy? You shouldn't be out here in the orange grove. I'll bet you're not over fifteen, are you? Are you in school regularly?"

"I've been working or looking after my sister since I was ten," Roy answered. "Dad says I can start again this year. We'll see."

"How much did you make today, son?"

"Eighty-eight cents."

"And Mr. Landon here made a little over a dollar, is that right?"

"I guess. He didn't say."

"And Ted here didn't make anything."

"It wasn't because I didn't want to," Ted protested.

"You're right," Peter Barlow said. "I hear the same thing everywhere. You try, but it doesn't get you anywhere. Whatever you do, it's not enough. That's what

120

I've been telling the men at the campsites. Mark my words, you'll be at two cents a basket tomorrow. They'll take most of you now for a while, but you'll be paid less. The growers have you men by the short hairs and they're not going to let go. You can count on that, they're not going to let go."

24

"You're back again today, are you, kid?" Mr. Sykes stopped next to Roy for a second. He put his hand on Roy's shoulder and moved on to Walt Landon. "And we'll take your father, too."

"He's not my father," Roy said.

"No matter, we'll take him. He's a good worker like you." Sykes laughed.

A voice from the end of the line called, "What are you paying today?"

"That's a good question," Sykes replied.

"What about an answer? Yesterday you dropped the pay to two and a half cents. Are you going to drop it again today?"

Roy turned to see who was demanding answers from Mr. Sykes. It was the big rugged farmer who had argued with Sykes the evening before. Later he had been in the grandstand with his kids. Roy hadn't seen the mother. The oldest girl seemed to be tending to the younger children.

Sykes went up to the farmer who had challenged him.

George—that was the name of the man with the club—was a step behind, the black nightstick in his hand.

"It's you again, Wilder, is it?" Sykes said. "You're not going to find out until one of the pickers tells you tonight. I don't want to see you here tomorrow morning. I've already told you once. We don't allow Reds in the orchard. All aboard," he shouted to the men he had selected.

"Reds, that's what they call men who ask questions," Ted whispered to Walt and Roy.

"He sounded like a man out of work to me, like the rest of us," Walt said. "I heard his wife died about the same time he lost his farm. He came out here from Iowa."

It seemed to Roy that the work was harder and longer than yesterday. He figured he didn't have time to *walk* back into the orchard after he lugged his basket to the checker. The picking was getting farther away. Now he ran, canvas bag flapping at his side. Only the really old men walked, he noticed, stumbling over the uneven ground and sometimes tripping on the fallen oranges. One old man, frail and tottering, bent over and leaned against a tree. "I'm all right," he told a picker who stopped. "You go on, I'm catching my breath." He sank to the ground, his back against the trunk. When Roy returned that way, the old man was gone. He looked for him on the truck in the evening; the man wasn't there.

They had cut the rate to two cents a basket. Roy shook his head in disappointment. He had picked a lot more fruit, he was sure. He handed the ninety cents to Walt Landon. "I tried hard today," he said. "I can't do any more than what I did today."

"It ain't your fault, Roy. Like Hank said they would, they're playing games with us. You'd think they'd treat grown men with more respect. They don't give a darn for us."

"They're selling oranges for a penny apiece, Emily told me," Ted said. "We get two pennies for picking a whole basket. Something is mighty wrong. These growers are getting rich while they starve us."

"You don't have to be a Red to figure that out," Walt said. "They tell me you can do better in the fields, but it's harder work, on your knees or bent over all day. Looks like you can't win. Do you and Harlow want to eat with us tonight, Roy? Mother said she'd cook up a mess of rice and beans with fatback if she got to the store."

"No, thanks. We have some bread and cold cuts left. We better eat them up before they go bad."

Mary was sitting on the Reo's running board. "Your dad's gone off," she announced to Roy. "He said to tell you he was starting work sooner than he thought."

Roy felt a surge of disappointment. All day long in the orchard, even when he was ready to drop in the middle of the afternoon, he kept thinking of how he didn't want to leave the fairgrounds. It wasn't only because of Mary, either, though she was mostly why he wanted to stay. He felt more at home with the Wheelers and the Landons than he did with Dad. It was like how he felt with Mr. Whitlock and Maynard. They were sort of his relatives. With Dad, he was just tagging along, looking after him maybe, but mainly hoping Dad didn't get drunk and waiting for him to do something worthwhile.

"Who'd he go off with, Mary?"

124

"A man in a black car came looking for him. He knew where your dad was supposed to be. He was one of those security people Pa told us about. He had a club in his belt. Is your father going to work for them?"

"That's what he says. He didn't want to pick oranges because he thought it might make them not hire him. When did he say he'd be back?"

"All he said was to tell you he'd be along to fetch you as soon as he could. You're used to looking after yourself, I've noticed," Mary remarked. "Was your dad away a lot when you were growing up?"

"A whole lot," Roy answered. "Do you want a baloney sandwich for supper? I have some left from the store."

"I'd like that," Mary said. "We could sit right here and eat our supper. I'll bring out a plate of beans while you get the water. We'll have ourselves a picnic, Roy."

Martha Landon had only one extra plate. She gave her daughter two forks. "You can eat off one side and Roy the other. I don't reckon he has any germs you don't have. Are you a little bit stuck on Roy, child?"

Mary lowered her head. "I don't know, Ma. A little, I guess. No boy ever paid attention to me before. He seems more like a brother than anything."

"He's going off with his father," Martha said.

"I know, Ma, but it won't hurt if we have a picnic by the truck, will it? Or if we go to the grandstand to count the stars?"

"No, Mary, it won't hurt," Martha said sadly. "The good Lord knows it won't hurt."

A single bean remained on the cracked plate. "It's

yours, Roy." Mary laughed. "I've been counting and it's yours."

"It's not mine," he protested. "I took the last forkful. I left that one for you."

"It's yours, anyway. I don't want it."

"We'll divide it up," Roy said. He cut the bean in half with his fork. He picked up one half and held it out for Mary, then took the other half for himself. "You sit here, I'll go wash the plate and forks and we'll go along to the grandstand. Is your leg all right?"

"It doesn't pinch so much. Ma says exercise helps me get used to the brace."

Peter Barlow was talking earnestly to a group of men on the bottom plank of the grandstand. He nodded to Roy. "You went to work today?" he asked.

"Yeah," Roy replied. "Mary's dad, too, and Ted Wheeler—all three of us."

"They need everyone they can hire now just about," Barlow said. He went back to talking to the men, one of whom was the big farmer Sykes had called a Red.

"When do you suppose your father's coming for you?" Mary asked.

"Soon, I reckon. We'll be in Riverside, he says. That's not far away."

"You'll be in school, won't you?"

"That's what Dad says. We'll see each other there every day."

"No, we won't. Ma says the kids from the fairgrounds and the campsites don't go to school. You have to be part of the town and have a house or something. They don't have places for pickers' kids. No school buses, either."

"Oh," Roy said. Down in front, Mr. Barlow was squatting in front of the men. "You have to act together," he was saying, "not just some of you, but all of you. You have to go hungry together, look after yourselves together, and say no to the Association together. They'll do anything to get you to work right now. We're coming to the height of the season. They can't afford to lose the crop. They'll double or triple the pay. Then when you're back, they'll cut it to a penny. You have to hang together no matter how much it hurts."

Roy took Mary's hand. "Did you hear that, Mary? It sounds like he's talking about us—Ted and Emily and your parents and even Frankie. And me, too," he said fiercely. "Me, too. I'm not going to be left out."

25

A black car followed the truck as it rolled through the gate. The men unloaded, grumbling about what they had received for the day's work. Ted had made under a dollar. His canvas bag had split, and the checker had docked him fifty cents for a replacement. "They wouldn't even let me bring it home for Emily to sew up this evening," he told Walt and Roy.

A voice from the car called, "Roy." The boy turned to see his father leaning out the car window, beckoning for him to come. He walked slowly to the car.

"They told you I got the job, did they?" Harlow asked. "And an apartment, too, in Riverside. It's got a kitchen and a room for you. The woman who runs it says the school is three blocks away. Come on, get in. We'll drive down to pick up your bag."

Harlow stepped out to let Roy squeeze into the backseat. He had on black pants and a white shirt, a badge pinned to the pocket with California Protection Agency stamped on it. The driver, Roy saw, was the man who had been with Mr. Sykes that morning, the second man.

The man with the club *and* the holster. He gave Roy a glance of recognition.

"Come on, son, get in. Eddie will take us to town."

Roy stepped back. His father was one of them now, the men in the black pants and white shirts and felt hats. "I'll walk down to get my things," he said. "You wait here."

"I thought that was Harlow in the car," Walt said. "He got his job, did he? Good. This is no place for a boy who should be in school. The same with Mary. Mother and I are moving out of here soon as we can."

"He's gone to work for the Association," Roy said. "He's one of those security guards, I think, the ones they say beat people up. The driver was the one with the pistol at the pick-up this morning."

"It's a steady job," Ted said. "It ain't you that's working for them, it's your dad. The time's not far off, I can tell you, when I'd take that job for myself if they was to offer."

Roy looked Ted straight in the face. "You wouldn't, you know you wouldn't, not after seeing how they treat us."

"I'm not sure, Roy. When you're broke, you don't have any choice sometimes. I'd be doing it for Emily and Frankie."

Mary limped up to greet them. "Ma's got supper ready. Don't you want to wash up?"

Walt and Ted headed for the latrine. "What's the matter, Roy?" Mary asked.

"My dad came to get me. He's out by the gate. I didn't want him to come down here so you all could see him. He's one of them now."

129

"One of who?"

"One of those men who tell us what to do, who cheat us every chance they get, one of those security guards the Association hires. You know who I mean."

"You don't want to go with your dad?"

Roy shook his head. "He was in jail," he blurted, "for something he didn't do, but it changed him. He's been different since they turned him loose. I can't tell you how, but he's different. He doesn't care what he does any longer."

"Maybe you shouldn't go for a while," Mary said. "You can stay here with us until you see how it turns out. You can go live with him later, can't you?"

Roy hadn't thought of that. Mary was right. He'd stay on where he was for a spell, he decided. He was big enough to look after himself. On Sundays when he wasn't working he would hitch a ride into Riverside and spend the day with Dad. Later on, he'd see. Maybe Dad would find himself another job.

The black car eased down the road and stopped beside the Reo. "You ready yet?" Harlow shouted. "I have a meeting tonight. Grab your bag and jump in."

"I'm not going, Dad. I've been thinking that I have a job picking every day now and I sort of like living here. I don't want to leave right away. Maybe in a while when school starts."

Harlow crawled out of the front seat. He looked bigger in the white shirt and badge than Roy had ever seen him. He had a stick in his belt, too, that Roy hadn't noticed. "Don't be dumb, Roy. You don't want to stay here with these hicks. You'll all be out of a job in three weeks or a month. There's a bunch of Reds telling the pickers what to think. They're riding for a fall."

"That's your job now, is it?" Roy heard himself say. "You and Sykes and the others, you're hurting people who only want to earn a living." He remembered what Hank and Peter Barlow had said. "All you want to do is help the Association cheat us. I'm not going, you hear, I'm not going." Roy crawled into the back of the truck. "And you're not going to make me."

Harlow said something to the driver. Eddie got out of the car. He was bigger than Dad. He didn't have the holster on his belt, but he didn't look as though he would need it. The two men came toward the Reo.

"Come along, Roy," Harlow said one more time. "Don't make any more fuss. You're under age, and I'm your father. The law says you have to be with me."

"Just like the law said you had to go to jail," Roy shouted. He remembered Dad taking the last of his money. "What does the law say about you spending the money I earned on drink? That was stealing."

"They don't care about that, boy," Harlow said roughly. "You get out of that truck or we'll come up there and pull you out."

Roy didn't answer. Like a trapped animal, he shoved himself deeper into the corner. He lifted his feet to kick anyone who came close.

Harlow swung himself into the truck, followed by Eddie.

"You better wait, Harlow," Roy heard a voice say. "The boy don't want to go with you right now. We'll look after him for you until he's ready, won't we, Ted? He'll be all right with us."

131

Eddie turned around. "Out of the way, Grandpa. Mister Purdy wants his boy, and he's going to have him."

Walt took a step back. "We'll need some help, Hank!" he shouted into the shadows.

From between the cabins, Hank and a handful of men appeared. "You two men aren't allowed beyond the pick-up station. Those are the rules," Hank warned. "I'm in charge here. I'm telling you to go. Anything that happens after this will be your responsibility."

"You watch what you're saying," Eddie threatened. "We don't want any trouble with you stinking farmers."

Hank went to the truck. "Do you want to go with these men, Roy?"

Roy stood up. "No," he said. "Not now or ever. I'm staying right here. This is where I belong."

"You heard him," Hank said. "Now get in your car and leave."

26

Mary was washing breakfast dishes in a basin outside the cabin when she saw Roy walking back from the pick-up station.

"What's the matter?" she asked. "Are you sick?"

Roy shook his head.

"How come you didn't go with the others? Pa said they'd take everybody this morning. I haven't seen anyone coming back except you."

"They didn't take me," Roy answered. Mr. Sykes had come down the line, the way he always did, picking every man, it seemed like, until he came to Roy. Behind him was Eddie. "That's his boy," he said in a loud whisper.

"Not today, kid," Mr. Sykes said. "You don't need to come back tomorrow either." Before Roy could say anything except "But," the foreman had passed to the end of the line and shouted, "All aboard, we have some oranges to pick."

"Do you reckon it was your dad?" Mary asked. "I bet

133

he's determined to put you in school. He's probably sorry for what happened last evening."

"It was him all right, him and that Eddie guy. Tomorrow I'll walk down the road to another pick-up where they don't know me."

"They'll know you at the orchard," Mary pointed out.

"Not if I go to another orchard. There are lots of them around here."

Mary picked a cup from the soapy water and dried it off. "I'll bring you a cup of coffee. Ma said it was the last we had. It won't be hot, but you can have it." She returned with half a cup of thick black coffee. "I've been thinking. If you were to live with your dad, you might persuade him to find another job. Anyway, you'd be living in town in a regular house with water and a bathroom like we had on the farm. It wouldn't be so bad here if—"

"I'm not leaving, Mary. I learned from Mr. Whitlock and Maynard you're better off where they like you. I was real happy at the boat shed, even though they teased me because I was the youngest. I've been worrying about how I went off without having a chance to say good-bye to them. I feel bad about that."

"You could write them a letter and mail it to them."

"I can't write so good," Roy replied. "I can read all right, but I didn't get around to writing much before I left school."

"I can help you," Mary said. "Mrs. Tibbets said I had the best hand in the whole school. Ma brought some writing paper with us. We can write your Mr. Whitlock a nice letter together. It will give us something to do. It's pretty quiet when the men are gone."

134

"I'd like that," Roy said. "I'll get the water for your mother." He took the bucket from inside the door and headed for the water pipe. Hank was there talking to several women waiting to fill their buckets. "You taking the day off, Roy?" he asked.

"Naw, they won't have me anymore. They must figure I don't need a job with Dad working."

"You're staying on here, are you?" Hank said sympathetically. "But don't forget they have good schools in Riverside if you change your mind. I learned a lot there."

Roy moved uneasily to the pipe. He didn't think much of everyone telling him what was best for him. He turned on the tap. "After a spell, I'll move to town. I'll see what happens here first."

"I can tell you now what's going to happen here," Hank said. "I was just telling Laura and Kate the Association is closing down the campsites. The land belongs to the orchard owners. They've told everyone to be off before sunset."

"Why?" Roy asked. "Those people have no place to go, I heard."

"Some of the men went on strike yesterday. I guess you could call it a strike. They've been listening to Peter and talking among themselves, and about half of them didn't show up yesterday morning. Sykes said if they didn't show up this morning, they'd all have to get off the land. Peter just told me no one, not a single man, showed up this morning. He's in the office talking to Kevin. It's a strike, sure enough."

"What about the men here?" Roy asked.

"They'll have to decide for themselves. Mostly you're

135

new arrivals. The Association must figure they can use you to break the strike. Meanwhile we have to get ready here to take in the folks from the campsites. They're moving in here, most of them. This is state land; the owners can't throw them out of here. Do you want to help me?"

"Sure. What do I do?"

"Help me to stake out places for them to settle in. The women are helping, too. Kevin said to put as many as we can in the infield. The rest we'll tuck somewhere. Come along. I have some stakes in the barn. I'll show you how to pace off the sections. It will be crowded by nightfall."

Roy and the women gathered armfuls of stakes. "You mark off ten big paces—that's about thirty feet each way. I'll be back with some string. Right now I have to put someone at the gate to tell the new people where to go."

"Mary would like to do that," Roy told them. "She wants to feel useful."

"Good idea," Hank said. "I'll ask Martha to take charge of the cookhouse."

Within an hour the first families arrived at the gate in an old Ford truck whose tires were almost flat from the weight of people and their possessions. "Where to, ma'am?" a grizzled farmer at the wheel asked Mary.

"Down the road to the end of the racetrack. Someone there will show you."

"I'll let everyone out and make another trip or two," the man said. "Some of our friends have had to sell their cars. They didn't count on having to leave."

"If you want help, look for Hank. He's the man in a checkered shirt."

A few minutes later, another truck arrived, followed by a wheezing brown sedan. The first truck came back to the gate, Roy waving from the front seat. "I'm going to help load," he cried. "Emily will be up in a while to spell you. Frankie's taking his nap. Hank said to keep count of the people coming through."

"Hank doesn't have to tell me. I was already doing it," Mary shouted back. "Should I count you, Roy?"

Albert, the weatherbeaten man who drove the truck, and Roy made three trips before sunset. At the campsites, the families were waiting for them, their belongings piled neatly beside the dirt road and their children waiting nervously next to them. Without a word they helped Roy and Albert load the truck and climbed in back.

"They're mad," Albert said. "They ain't talking much but you can tell: They'll starve, every last one of them, before they'll go back. They sent a man in this morning as we were packing up, the Association did, to say we could stay and they would pay two and a half cents a basket. You know what they were paying yesterday? One and a half cents. You done any picking?"

"Three days," Roy said.

"How much did you make yesterday?"

"Seventy cents."

"You know what I'm talking about, then. And you don't have no kids either, I bet. That Barlow fellow told us to expect something like that. He was right. First they tell you to get off, then they start to play games with you. Our minds were made up by then. Some of us have been there for three years or more, just hanging on. They can't save the crop unless they can get people in.

137

We figure if everybody stays out, we have a chance to win this time."

"You've been on strike before?" Roy asked.

"Two years ago. It wasn't a real strike, I reckon. Some men stayed out. The Association threatened to close the site. At the same time they raised the rate half a penny. We went back. A couple of days after that, they cut it a penny a basket to pay for the fruit they lost when we struck, they said."

"It's going to be different this year?"

"You're darned right it's going to be different," Albert replied. "There's nothing for us now if it ain't."

27

By evening the infield was completely filled. Kevin Olsen and Hank put the last arrivals into whatever space they could find between the cabins or beyond the barn in the dirt parking lot.

"How many people did we take in?" Hank asked Mary.

"I counted seven hundred and twelve people altogether," she replied. "I might have missed a few kids hunkered down in the trucks."

"I wonder what we're going to do with them all. We must have over twelve hundred folks in here now," Hank remarked. "It's an awful strain on the latrine and the cookhouse. The first thing to do is shut the gate and put a man there around the clock. Sooner or later the Association will come calling."

"Are the men here going on strike?" Mary asked.

"I can't tell you, Mary. They'll have to decide that tonight. There's a meeting in the barn."

Roy recognized most of the men standing, sitting, or squatting in the barn. They had been in the lineup and in the truck bouncing along the dirt road to the orchard. Peter Barlow began to talk, explaining that he and his friends had been working with the pickers in the three campsites for the last several years. He knew the men and their families there; now he was getting around to the pickers in the fairgrounds. "You are new arrivals," he said, "but already you are in the same boat with those people who came to the valley earlier. Let me ask you how much did they pay you today for a basket of oranges?"

"Three cents," a man up front responded.

"And yesterday, how much?"

"Two cents."

"Why do you think the growers were so generous today and so mean yesterday?" Barlow went on.

No one answered.

"And how much do you reckon you'll get for picking a basket of their oranges if all the other men decide suddenly to go to work tomorrow?"

Mumbles and murmurs in the crowd, but no response.

"Well, I'll tell you, and if I'm wrong you can make me eat a basket of oranges. One and a half cents a basket, maybe only a penny if they think they can get away with it. Right now they need you to break the strike. They'll pay you up to five cents a basket if they have to."

"You mean," one voice asked, "we might get five cents a basket if we keep working?"

"Sure, you can," Barlow responded. "Will you share it with the families outside who make it possible?"

"That's not our business," the voice argued. "I have my own family to look after. If they don't want to work, it ain't my fault."

"Who are you, anyway?" another man shouted from the back of the barn. "You brought all these strikers here to where we live. There ain't hardly no room for them here."

"I brought them here, Phil," Kevin Olsen said, "just like I brought you here a while back when you had nowhere to go. The growers threw these folks off the land when they went on strike."

"You had no business doing that without asking us."

Walt Landon rose to his feet. He addressed the angry man in back of him. "I don't know your name, friend, but we've picked together the last couple of days and I've seen you and your family at your tent. I'd say that makes us neighbors. Back home when there was a fire or a tornado, the neighbors all got together to help the folks that were distressed. The way I see it, all of us are in trouble together. None of us has a place to go. The only jobs we have are what the Association lets us have. I say we better share what we have and do what we have to do together to see us through."

Barlow went on in his calm persuasive voice. "If you all want more or less regular wages, you are going to fight for them, not beg. Your friends out there are on strike. The question is, do you want to take advantage of them or do you want to join them? I honestly believe you men can win this time. You have a chance to tell the Association you have rights, too. You can tell them to deal with you honestly."

Another man spoke up. "Who are you to tell us what to do? I've heard you are one of those Reds who want to take over the country."

"I am Peter Barlow. I am a lawyer and I work for a

union. As I see it, the union is for the farm workers like the Association is for the growers. You don't have to join the union to go on strike. If you lose, you're not going to join anyway, but if you win, you may want to join. That will be your business. I'm not what you call a Red, unless you say voting for President Roosevelt is being a Red. If that's what you mean, there must be a whole lot of Reds in this country. I can tell you who the growers voted for."

Ted stood up. "What are you asking us to do?"

"No more than what the pickers at the campsites did, take a strike vote."

"You mean, we vote to join them or to go to work tomorrow?"

"Yes," Barlow said. "That's all there is to it."

"And if we don't go to work, what then?" a man squatting in front of Barlow demanded.

"You'll have to suffer hard times; your wife and kids, if you have any, will be hungry. You'll hurt and you'll get angry and you'll want to do something. But you will have to be patient and wait. That's all."

"What will we get if we win?"

"I can't tell you exactly. You will have to elect some of your people to a committee to talk to the Association's people. We'll help you. The growers won't want to deal with a union and they won't want to make a contract with the pickers. At first they will offer you a guarantee of so much a basket for the rest of this season and a promise to talk about other things you want later on. But all that is down the road. First they'll try to break the strike any way they can. You have to get them to negotiate. I think I've said everything I came here to say. I'm going outside now. You decide what you want to do."

The men were quiet for a while, waiting for someone to start the discussion. "I reckon I'll go outside, too," Roy said. "I'm not old enough to vote."

"If you're old enough to work, you're old enough to vote," Walt said.

"But they won't let me work," Roy said.

"Did Sykes let me work the first day I showed up?" Walt reminded him. "And did they let Ted work the next day?" Mr. Landon's voice rose in anger. He stood up. "I don't know about the rest of you, because I've been here only a week or so, but I'm going to vote with the strikers. It's no more than fair.

"I had a farm until the bank took it from me, and if you'd asked me then about a union or a strike, I would have told you I'd drop dead before I'd join a union or go strike. I'm not a farmer now and neither is none of you. You're just someone with a pair of hands and a strong back the Association can use when it needs you. The only thing you have now is your labor, and it seems to me Mr. Barlow has told you it has some value if you use it right. All of us may have farms or jobs again when good times return, but right now we don't have any choice. We better do the right thing together, not one by one. That's all I have to say."

"I agree with that," an old man said. "We can't be much worse off than we are. I want to ask Kevin Olsen a question. Can we stay here? You ain't going to throw us off if we go on strike, are you?"

Kevin moved to the front from the side of the barn

where he had been listening. "No. The Association will try to see to it that you can't remain, but I have word from the governor's office that you can stay. The grounds belong to the state, not the county. But you'll have to look after yourselves. Hank and I will be here if you need us."

For an hour the talk went back and forth, not so much people arguing, Roy thought, as talking themselves into something. When the voices were still, the big man who had stopped at the checker's table to count the coins in his hand, Tobias Wilder, moved to the front. "It's time for a vote, I'd say. Why don't those of you in favor of going on strike move to the right. Those of you who want to keep on working, move to the left."

Walt and Roy and Ted moved directly to the right. One by one the pickers stood up, looked at each other, shrugged, and joined them. No one moved to the left.

"There ain't no need to count," Tobias Wilder said. "We got ourselves a strike."

28

"We'll put men at the gate around the clock," Hank said. "There will be some rough stuff, I'll bet on it. Two years ago the security goons came into one of the sites at night and beat up three men who had spoken against the Association. That helped scare the rest of the pickers. This isn't their property, but they are bound to try something."

"I'll take the first shift," Walt said.

"I'll go with you," Tobias Wheeler said. "Matty can look after the little ones."

"Here's the key to the padlock," Hank said. "Put the chain on and lock it. Pass the key on to the men who relieve you. Tomorrow we'll form committees to keep things running smooth. I can tell you it's going to be a problem finding food for all the people inside here."

"What happened, Roy?" Mary asked when Roy came from the barn. "It's too late to go to the grandstand, I bet. You were in there an awful long time."

"Maybe Emily and Ted will want to go. What the men did was vote for a strike. They talked about Reds and such, but when it came right down to it, they all voted to stay out until they got proper pay. They talked about some other things I didn't understand, like contracts and unions and stuff, but what they want now is the Association to guarantee them so much a basket. I think they have three cents a basket in their minds. Your dad is going up to the gate to see that Sykes and his men don't get in to cause more trouble."

"What about your dad, Roy?"

"Dad's not going to bother us," Roy said loyally. "Mr. O'Neill must have a lot of things he can set Dad to doing."

"I'll ask Ma and Ted and Emily if they want to walk around to the grandstand. Listen, Roy, you can hear them singing over there."

"They want to keep their spirits up, I reckon. Mr. Barlow said a strike wasn't any picnic. It will be a rough time for all of us and we'll have to hang together. Get the others and we'll go listen."

Mary limped back from her cabin.

"Frankie and Ted are asleep, and Ma is tuckered out. She says we should go anyway by ourselves," Mary reported. "But we can't stay too long. You take my arm, and we'll hurry along."

The grandstand was half-filled. In the infield, a group of the newcomers—men, women, and children—were singing old favorite songs that Roy remembered from the Fourth of July picnic the Methodist church in Tilson held every year. A man who looked like a preacher stood in front of the group waving his arms and shouting out the name of the song they were to sing next.

Roy sat close to Mary, his arm lightly around her waist, the way Ted sat next to Emily. Mary rested her head on Roy's shoulder and hummed along with the singers.

When the singing was finished, the preacher man walked to the infield fence. "We want to thank you for joining us," he shouted to the grandstand. "Together we are going to win." The people in the stands stood up. "We're going to win," they cheered, "we're going to win."

"God bless you," the preacher shouted. "Let's all of us sing together 'The Old Rugged Cross.' We'll see you here tomorrow night."

Roy lay back in the truck. The cool night air was settling over the campground. He pulled the old quilt Dad had been using up over his chest. He rubbed his cheek where Mary had brushed her lips when he left her at the cabin door. Everything was happening too fast for him to keep track of. It seemed that his life was changing from day to day, not only with Mary but with Dad and everyone around him. He supposed that's what growing up was about. He was fifteen now and probably would never go to school again, so he must be almost grown up. Maynard used to brag that he hadn't been to school after the third grade. Mr. Whitlock always stopped whatever he was doing to comment, "Well, take a good look at yourself now, Maynard. You aren't much to be proud of."

Roy remembered that Maynard had married when

he was seventeen. "I've been regretting it ever since, Roy," he said. "You be sure not to be as mule dumb as I was, no matter how many pretty looks Lucy gives you."

Mr. Whitlock shook his head. "Don't you be listening to him, Roy. Maynard here's been married to Alva thirty years, and he wouldn't part with her for all the money in the First National Bank."

Did Mary think they were going steady? She had told him her mother was glad she and Roy liked each other so much. What was going to become of Mary? There wasn't much for her to do, she complained, until Walt found them a little farm where she could go to school and have her chickens and maybe sell the eggs in town. "I'm not ever going to be much use to anyone, Roy," she told him.

It probably didn't make any difference anyway how he felt about Mary Landon. You didn't have to be a genius to know that Dad wasn't going to let him go on living in the fairgrounds. Maybe Dad couldn't do anything now, what with the strike to keep him busy and the gate locked to keep Sykes's men out, but when it settled down, Dad would be back to get him, maybe with the police. Or he might sneak over the fence out beyond the parking lot with George or Eddie and carry him off. Roy shivered at the thought. If he slept under the truck on that old piece of canvas Mr. Landon had, they wouldn't find him. He'd do that soon as they had won the strike.

Three cents a basket, and no charge for the ride to the orchards and back, that's what the men were talking about. And nothing for the shoulder bag, either, especially if the pickers brought their own. Some of the women had said they would sew bags for their husbands. Maybe Mary could sew one for him if the canvas wasn't too thick.

Roy thought of the first doll Dad had made for Lilian. He hadn't told Mary about her. He felt sorry for his father. If he could sew dolls, he could make shoulder bags too and join Ted and Walt and the others. He had no business riding around the orchards in a black car, no business at all. That made him a goon.

Three cents a basket. Roy started to do the figures. Thirty cents to start with that he didn't get now. Plus about sixty baskets, which was what he picked the last day, maybe more if they moved the checker closer to where the picking was, which was what some men wanted. He counted the baskets off on his fingers. Why, it came to over two dollars if he hadn't made a mistake. Just what he earned at the boat shed, two dollars, but that was for regular skilled work, not picking oranges off a tree. He would give Mr. Landon a dollar every day until he figured he had paid his and Dad's way to California. He'd have a dollar left to save and buy Mary a really nice birthday present.

First, they had to win the strike. Singing songs at night wasn't going to do the trick. Mr. Barlow hadn't even promised outright that they would win. And he had said there would be trouble sooner or later. The pickers would show the goons a thing or two, Roy thought, when it came to that. The big man with the kids, Toby, looked strong enough to take on three of them at a time. He hoped Dad would stay out of it. He had no business getting hurt. He wasn't really one of Sykes's men.

Through half-closed eyes Roy counted the stars. There had to be millions and millions up there. The night before last, he and Mary had started to count, taking turns. They were over three hundred before they gave up. "We'll never finish," Mary said, "even if we count the rest of our lives." She had laughed, nervouslike. "You know what I mean, Roy, don't you?"

29

"The union can give you some help, but it can't feed you," Peter Barlow told the men and women on the strike committee. "Hank tells me his brother has a dairy farm and will give him milk for the children. There are about twelve hundred people in the campground now. What do you plan to do?"

"We can hold out for a while," Walt Landon said. "Those of us who have a little money will share it."

"That won't get you far," Kevin Olsen said. "The state officials say you can stay here as long as there's no sanitation problem or a spreading sickness. But if they see starving kids, they'll have to step in. The growers know that, too. They'll try to wait you out."

"At first," Barlow said, "it will be a test of wills between the Association and the strikers. I can't really say who has the advantage."

"How long can the oranges wait?"

Hank responded, "They'll have to start picking some pretty soon if they're going to ship them east. When they fell behind two years ago, they had to put some women to work. They don't like to do that."

"I calculate in about a week they'll make their first move," Barlow said. "In about two weeks, they'll start to lose some of the crop. They probably count on holding out until then. Unless . . ."

"Unless what?" Walt asked.

"Unless they figure out some other way to deal with you. You must understand these are tough people, the growers and the security company. They have told themselves they can't afford to lose a strike. Not so much because of the union; we're just getting started and aren't any serious threat to them yet. It's more the idea that you men and women are free to strike. The way they look at it, you people ought to work on their terms. If you win the strike, you will be telling the pickers and field-workers all over the state that they can fight back, too."

A woman with a tent full of children, whom Kevin had asked to take charge of the milk distribution, spoke out angrily. "Why don't they sit down and talk it over with us and make an arrangement that's good for them and good for us? We aren't Reds. There ought to be something we can all agree on. I don't feel right being a striker."

"The Association doesn't see it that way, Mrs. Granger, and they know how most of you people feel. That gives them a big advantage. They really want to keep you weak," Peter Barlow said. "Our job now is to figure out how to find enough food to keep you going. Any ideas, Mr. Landon?"

"I was talking to my wife and the people we share the

cabin with. It does appear to us there's food out there if we can just get it somehow. I mean, it ain't like it was back home, where everything just dried up on you. This is rich country in the valley. We thought . . . well, we probably didn't know what we were saying, being as how we just arrived."

"Why don't you tell us, Mr. Landon?" Kevin said.

"I'm a little bit ashamed, I guess. What it amounts to is begging, or if you want to put it another way, asking folks who live nearby to share with us for a while until we can get on our feet. Some of the Californians who live here must wish we had stayed where we came from. That's natural, I suppose, unless you've seen a whole state, and other states, too, turn to dust and blow away. Then you might understand why we came to California. They tell me some folks think we are Reds who came all the way from Russia."

"That's about it, Mr. Landon," Kevin said. "Still, you have some support. Why don't you give it a try? Take a couple of kids with you in the truck, Mary and Roy there, Mrs. Wheeler and her baby, to let them know who the people in the fairgrounds really are, what they look like, that they're people just like themselves."

Roy spoke up. "Back home, the American Store put its produce that was spoiled or almost spoiled at the back of the store at night. Two-day-old bread they hadn't sold, too. Sometimes when Ruth Ann didn't have any money, I'd stop by to help myself if there was something we could use. Maybe they do the same here."

"It's no time to be proud," Walt said. "We can try that, if the stores don't have any objection."

"Keep at least two men at the gate on shifts," Kevin

153

told Toby. "If they bring in goons they'll try to come in that way. They won't break through the fence around the fairgrounds. That would be trespassing and destruction of state property. The Association doesn't want to start a fight with the state of California.

"I guess that's about it. Hank and I can't be part of the strike. Our job is to look after the property and help people in distress. We work for the state. I can tell you the local authorities won't be sympathetic with you, don't forget that. They support the growers because they know them. They also don't want trouble. So don't do anything wrong when you leave the grounds. If the police for some reason tell you to do something, you'd be smart to do it. A strike gets everybody mad with the strikers. And inside here, we absolutely must keep everything clean and tidy. The Association will have inspectors in here soon enough."

"Let's go," Walt said to Mary and Roy. "We might as well make a trip to Cordelia. I'll ask Ted to get the Reo started up for us and if we can borrow Emily and Frankie for the morning. You two can ride in the back."

Ted climbed into the cab. "We haven't turned her over since we arrived," he said. "I have a feeling the battery may have worn out along with everything else." He jammed his boot on the starter. Not a sound from under the hood. Ted sighed and got out to lift the hood. "The connections are okay. I think it's dead. We're on a slope here. We'll ask a couple of men to push us down toward the barn to see if it will catch."

Ted and Roy and two men from the next cabin pushed the Reo down the road. Walt slipped the gearshift into second and released the clutch. The truck groaned and turned over once. Walt put his foot on the clutch. When the Reo was rolling fast he released it once more. The Reo heaved and ground and sputtered and caught. Walt pulled out the throttle. "By golly, it worked," he said. "I won't turn her off until we come back."

"It will charge itself as you go along," Ted told him. "Park it on the slope when you come back. We'll have to keep her going until we win the strike. Then we'll trade her in for a new Cadillac. I'll ask Emily if she'll go along with you. Where are you going first?"

"I thought we'd talk to that nice lady at the Cordelia Café. They must have leftovers at the café, wouldn't you say, Roy? She's only the waitress, I know, but it wouldn't do no harm."

30

Mr. Landon agreed to try his hand first at collecting food at the Cordelia Café. If he wasn't successful, he said that Roy and Mary could give it a shot. "We'll save Frankie for last of all," he laughed. "No one's going to turn *him* down if Emily can get him to smile. You all can wait here in the truck, unless you want to come along, Roy, to help out if I forget what to say."

The waitress at the café who had sent them to the fairgrounds when they first arrived was sitting at the counter. "Hi," she greeted them. "Come have a cup of coffee on the house. How are you all getting along? I've been wondering about you. Where's the baby?"

"He's out in the truck with Emily. We'll ask her if he can come visit. He's got a new tooth. Go tell her to bring Frankie in, Roy."

"I'll get the coffee," the waitress said. "Pull up a stool."

"That's nice of you, ma'am," Walt said. "But the fact is, we came here for another reason. Have you heard about the strike?"

"Have I ever! The security men for the Association are in here a lot, those men in the white shirts. The growers are bringing in more of them. It's good business for Nick."

Roy came back carrying Frankie. "Emily has a cramp in her leg. You can hold Frankie awhile. The tooth is right here." He pulled Frankie's bottom lip down.

"Isn't he something?" the waitress said. "He came all the way across the country?"

"From Ohio," Walt said. "That's most of the country. Hitchhiking part of the way, his parents say, after the car gave out. He's a good boy, I can tell you."

"You men are on strike, too?" the waitress asked.

"Yeah," Roy answered proudly. "We're in charge of the food detail. Isn't that right?" he asked Mr. Landon.

"I was wondering why you're here. You haven't come to buy picnic lunches for the strikers, have you?"

"I reckon we didn't. You might say we came here to beg," Walt answered slowly. "Not for food, but scraps we can use that you throw out. We'd pick them up in the evenings."

The waitress made a face. "I don't know how Nick will feel about that. He has a lot of business from the farmers as well as the security men. All you can do is ask him. Nick!" she shouted toward the kitchen.

A dark-skinned man came through the swinging door, wiping his hands on an apron tied around his waist. "What you want?" he asked.

Linda nodded to Walt and Roy. Mr. Landon repeated what he had said to the waitress.

"No can help," Nick said abruptly. "The farm people, they come here to eat, not you people in old cars. No can help."

157

He spoke in a way Roy couldn't make out too well. "It's just leavings, mister. We're not beggars. If we made good money picking, we'd eat here, too. We're broke and hungry, mister."

"It's none of my business," Linda intervened, "but if you put what you don't use out in a box, Nick, they could pick it up after dark and make soup or something with it. No one would know. You have kids of your own like Frankie here. You wouldn't want them to starve."

Nick grimaced and clenched his hands again and again. "Okay, I do it. After dark, understand? If police catch you, say I said was okay." He looked at Frankie and smiled. "I was hungry in Greece. Turks burnt my village. Some us dead, my uncle and kids." He rubbed Frankie's head and returned to the kitchen.

"That was mighty good of him. Maybe it's our lucky day. Is there a bakeshop in town, ma'am?" Walt asked Linda.

"Just a little one. We get our bread and pastries from the Superior Bakery in Riverside. I don't know about them." Linda held Frankie out to Roy and went behind the counter. Two men came into the café, big men with brown felt hats and white shirts and black trousers. They looked hard at Roy and Walt and slumped over the counter. Roy and Walt left with Frankie.

"We did something, Mary," Roy reported. "The man—Nick—was tough at first, then he was real nice. You know what, Mary? He was a foreigner. From Greece, he said. Did they teach you where that is?"

"It's a really old country over in Europe. If I had a map, I could show you. Miss Watts showed us pictures of ruins and statues from back when Greece was important.

158

She said this was where all our learning started, from the Greeks. Where is Pa going now?"

"Over to Riverside. Linda, the waitress in the café, said it was a lot bigger than Cordelia. There's a bakery there that might give us day-old bread."

"I'll come in, too, this time. I like the smell of bread baking. I used to help Ma. She baked for the whole week on Saturday. She'd wrap the bread in wax paper and keep it in the bread box."

The owner of the Superior Bakery had his office in the back of the bakery next to the loading platform where drivers were carrying trays of bread and pastries to fill their trucks. He listened impatiently to Walt Landon and stared at the brace on Mary's leg.

"Look," he said when Walt had stumbled to the end of his speech. "I'm a business man, not a charity. Riverside used to be just a spot on the map until the growers and farmers and businessmen like me made it into a real town, almost a city. We're proud of what we've done, mister, and we don't need people like you out here. We were getting along just fine until you Okies—I guess that's what they call you—showed up. The Association gave most of you jobs until you took it into your heads to listen to some Red organizers and go on strike. What kind of gratitude is that? You won't get any bread from me, or anyone else in town, I can guarantee that."

"We aren't looking for charity, mister. We're willing to buy the returns and the leftovers. What do you call them, Roy?"

"Day-old bread, two-day-old bread, whatever he has he can't sell in the stores."

"That's it. Stale bread, I guess you'd call it."

159

The owner considered the matter. "You'd pick it up, would you? I'm not running a delivery service to the fairgrounds."

"Yes, sir, we'd pick it up."

"Sometimes there aren't many returns. You'd just have to take what I wanted to get rid of."

"Yes, sir," Walt agreed.

"And if the growers get on me, I'll have to stop. Still, I don't tell them how to sell their citrus; they oughten to be telling me how to run my bakery. One thing more, I'll want a deposit. You can work against that; when it's used up, I'll want another deposit. That's part of the deal. Stale bread isn't free, you know. I can always sell it to the pig farmers."

"Yes, sir, we're obliged to you." Walt folded a twenty-dollar bill. "Here's our deposit. We don't want to be a problem to people who live here. We're not bums, just folks like you who are down on our luck. We'd sort of like to be your neighbors."

"You're not neighbors, I can tell you that right now. You can buy and I can sell. But that doesn't make us neighbors. Come by tonight toward seven." He reached over to take the bill from Walt's fingers. "It will be sitting on the platform in big cardboard boxes."

31

"We didn't do very well," Walt reported to the food committee, "not good enough to feed more than a table of hungry relatives and the family dog. The grocery stores wouldn't talk to us. But a butcher did promise us a barrel of bones free every other evening. He'll keep them in the cold-storage room and put them out at closing time. We'll pick them up when we fetch the bread. You're in charge of reminding me when every other day is, Roy."

"I will," Roy promised.

Martha Landon spoke up. "We have some big pots in the cookhouse. We can use the bones to boil up a broth for the beans and rice. Mr. Barlow told us a union in San Francisco is sending down a truckload. They won't taste like much, but they'll keep us going."

"Some of us can slip out to the orchards and bring back oranges," Roy whispered to Hank. "It wouldn't be stealing if they was rotting on the ground, would it?"

"Some of you would get yourselves shot, too," Hank explained. "The Association has brought in twenty more

161

men, and I heard they're calling more down from the Bay Area. They'll put some in every orchard with guns, you can bet on that. You be careful, Roy. It looks like Walt and you are off to a good start. We won't starve the first week. My brother's giving us three cans of milk every morning, enough to take care of the kids."

"We'll have to be patient," Walt advised. "Let's just make our rounds in the Reo and see what happens. Some of the women are sewing canvas bags for the day we win the strike. You can help them, Mary, if you are of a mind to."

"Let me show you something, Mary," Roy said. He climbed up into the truck and took the odd-eyed doll from his bag. "Dad made this when he was in prison."

"Who was it for?" Mary asked.

"My half sister Lilian, but she didn't like the button eyes where they were and wouldn't play with her. I brought it along in case I see Lilian sometime and she changes her mind."

"I can fix the eyes, Roy."

Roy thought about it. That wouldn't be right, he decided. The doll reminded him of the way Dad used to be. He had been pretty good to them most of the time. "I reckon not," he said. "I sort of like her the way she is."

Mary took her. "She *is* kind of cute this way, isn't she? 'Mary Jane' is on her overalls. Is that her name?"

"Dad named her after the candy bar. I'll just call her Mary from now on. How about that?"

"You'll have two Marys, then, Roy," Mary Landon

said. She limped back to her cabin. "I have to help Ma now."

At noon on the fourth day, Peter Barlow called a meeting of the strike committee. "The Association has made its first move," he told them. "One of the growers looked me up in town and said both sides were being stubborn for no good reason. They had made some mistakes, according to him, and so had you. It was maybe time to get together. He thought it wouldn't be too much of a matter to settle the differences. Informally, he said he could get the Association members to listen if you men were disposed to go back to work. I'm supposed to tell you that."

"What about the pay?" Bob Tucker asked. He was in charge of the strike committee. He had owned a big grain company in Nebraska that went bust, Walt told Roy. After he paid off his debts, he joined the parade of farmers heading west. "He's an educated man, Roy, like your dad. He's been to college."

"He couldn't be sure," Barlow said, "but he thought he could get them to agree they wouldn't pay less than two cents a basket for the rest of the season."

Tucker looked around at the men on the committee. They shook their heads. "Should we spread the word and take a vote? It hardly seems necessary."

"Naw," one of the men said. "What do you think, Mr. Barlow?"

"I think they're anxious. It's not like the Association to make the first move so early. It's a good crop this year. They don't want to lose any of it."

"We'll wait," Tucker said. "If you see that man again,

163

you can tell him they'll have to do better than that. I have a feeling the men won't go back for less than three cents."

It was late when the meeting broke up. Walt and Roy went to the butcher shop first. They lifted three heavy tubs of bones into the truck and left the empty ones beside the back door of the butcher shop. They collected five boxes of bread from the bakery and, finally, two bags of assorted handouts from the Cordelia Café. It was pitifully little for twelve hundred people, Walt told Roy as they climbed into the truck. "I wish the Lord would come to visit and turn what we have into enough for the multitude. We're getting to the bottom of the bin."

It was about dark by the time they left Riverside. The Reo's dim lights covered only a small patch of road ahead of them. Mr. Landon watched a heavy truck rushing toward them. He gripped the steering wheel and slowed down. "What's that fool doing on the wrong side of the road?" he exclaimed. He eased the Reo's right wheels off the pavement. The truck pounded on, straight toward them. Its lights flashed on and off. Its horn blared. At the last second Mr. Landon swung the Reo out of its path into the ditch. Roy heard something crack underneath.

The other truck roared past. It moved over to the right side of the road and disappeared around a curve.

"He wanted to do that," Roy shouted. "He wanted to hit us or run us into the ditch."

Mr. Landon opened his door. He was shaking. "He wanted to do something all right, else he was crazy. I'm pretty sure the driver was in a white shirt. It might have

been one of Sykes's goons trying to do just what he did."
He kneeled to look at the front of the Reo tilted into the
ditch. "He done it all right. The axle is busted."

"Damn," Roy said. "Damn him to hell."

"No sense in swearing, Roy. It won't fix our truck.
You go on to the fairgrounds and tell Mr. Gurney to
come by in his pickup to move the food for us. I'll sit
here to see they don't come back and steal it."

When Mr. Gurney and Roy returned, Walt was sitting
dejected on the running board in the dark. "The police
patrol came by right after you left, Roy. They said I
couldn't leave my truck here. It was a safety hazard. You
can see how wrong they are; the Reo is ten feet or more
off the road. They're sending out a tow truck. It's going
to cost me fifteen dollars. That's the last of my money. It
must have been the man who drove me off the road who
put them up to it. Kevin said they would play tough, and
that's what they did. That's sure what they did."

The next evening Mr. Gurney and Roy returned
empty handed. They told Walt the baker said they had
used up the deposit, and that was the end of their business. The following evening the tub outside the butcher
shop was empty. They banged angrily on the back door.
No one answered. Two days later, Hank's brother said
he was sorry, but he would have to stop providing milk
for the strikers' children. "They threatened to drive him
out of business if he didn't stop," Hank reported.

The Association's offer was still good, Peter Barlow
reported, but his so-called friend in town said it might
not be good much longer. "He says they are bringing in
pickers from the north."

"Is he bluffing?" Tucker asked.

"I think so, but you had better not count on it. They already have security people doing some picking. It's just for show, but you ought to know you're coming down to the tough times now."

"We'll make the rounds and ask," Tucker replied. "But I can already tell you what their answer will be. The men are still mad."

32

The days passed slowly. Roy and Mary sat by the gate and counted cars. Among the vehicles that passed in the afternoon were school buses carrying children home to Cordelia. None of the kids inside waved to the people at the gate. An occasional picker whose car still worked left the campground to look for a job. He returned in the evening shaking his head to the men at the gate.

Down the slope dispirited women snapped at whining children. The men squatted in the shade pulling at the grass or drawing circles in the dirt. The voices that had sung so strongly the first night of the strike had faded to whispers, and on the ninth day no one gathered around the preacher at the infield railing. The few families who had a supply of rations ate them secretly in their tents at night or behind the closed doors of their cabins.

On the twelfth day, Peter Barlow told Walt Landon and Bob Tucker, "They can't take much more. I've been through a lot of strikes, and there comes a time when the spirit begins to break. I can see it happening here. These poor people had nothing to start with, most of them.

They were hungry when the strike began. They lived off the excitement for a while, that and being just plain mad at the growers."

"Where's that truck of rice and beans and corned beef?" Walt said. "It was supposed to be here three days ago, you said, Peter."

"I don't know. I talked to the union secretary in San Francisco. He said be patient, they are trying to round up the food. I think they're stealing it from warehouses. I don't ask and they don't tell me."

"How about the oranges?" asked Toby who came up to squat between Roy and Walt Landon.

"The Association is paying something extra to the goons to do the picking," Kevin said. "It's nowheres near enough, and it won't do the trick, but it gives the growers a few extra days. There's no talk in town about settling. They're going to try to wait the men out. Some of our pickers are beginning to weaken. They're blaming you, Peter, for taking them out."

"That's what always happens," Barlow said. "I'm the lightning rod."

"It ain't your fault," Toby said. "They're grown men, and they voted fair and square, every living one of them, to strike."

"I know," Barlow said, "but that's not the point. The women worry about the children. The men have nothing to do. They can't go and picket an orchard, so they have nothing to do but blame me. It's easier than blaming the growers. They know who I am. They don't know the growers. I suspect they'd take two cents a basket if the Association were to offer it right now."

A small crowd had gathered around the group. "Two

cents looks pretty good," the man commented. "It's better than the penny and a half they paid the day we quit."

"I won't go back," Roy said proudly. "If they hear you talk like that," he accused the man, "they'll offer you only a penny. Isn't that so, Mr. Barlow?"

The union man nodded.

"It's all right for you to talk that way, Roy," Mary snapped. "You can always go live with your dad in Riverside."

"Mary!" Martha Landon scolded. "That wasn't nice. You apologize to Roy."

"He knows I didn't mean it, Ma. My leg aches. I'm too tired to drag this heavy brace around. I wish we were still riding out to Riverside in the Reo collecting food and talking about winning. We aren't going to win, are we, Pa? What are you going to do then?"

"I don't know, Mary. I truly don't know. I hadn't planned on losing, honey. Most of the men and women—even their kids—are still strong. They won't give in. Peter says we aren't like factory workers. We're farmers mostly and we're used to being active and independent. We're not organized in our minds, he says, to do anything like go on strike."

"Come on, Mary, I'll walk you up to the gate," Roy said. "We can sit in the shade and count cars. Remember that yellow Stutz Bearcat that went whizzing by yesterday? I bet he was coming all the way from Los Angeles."

"Go on with Roy," Mary's mother said. "It won't do you any good lying around in the cabin. Frankie is cutting another tooth and he's as cranky as a hornet."

Mary was limping badly now. Roy walked slowly beside her. He wondered what she would do if he gathered

169

her in his arms and carried her up to the gate. He was strong enough to do it. He'd sweep her off her feet, brace and all, and she'd put her arms around his neck and tell him how strong he was and how proud she was of him. But he did nothing except take her elbow when one of the crutches slipped on a rock. He noticed that her face was twisted in pain and her hair damp with sweat.

"How about we stop for a minute and catch our breath?" he asked.

"No," Mary answered finally. "It's my problem, not yours. We'll rest at the gate." She plodded on, dragging the black boot in the dust.

The two men at the gate stared at the empty road. Roy didn't know their names. They clutched the wire mesh with fingers like parrots' claws, like some of the prisoners on the other side of the mesh in the visiting room at the Milford penitentiary.

Roy found their patch of grass under the eucalyptus trees. "Here's our place, Mary. We can see the cars fine from here."

"We could have brought a picnic lunch," Mary said, pulling her shirt down over her brace, "except . . ."

"Except that none of us has any bread or peanut butter or cold ham. Your ma says they're down to the last bag of rice in the cookhouse."

"I'm so tired of rice I can't eat it anymore," Mary explained. "It's all we have, but I'd rather starve. Look, here comes a car. What is it, Roy?"

"It's only a Ford roadster. See, it has a rumble seat. You see a lot of Fords on the road. Dad says if he had as much as Henry Ford, he'd know what to do with the money. But when I asked him what, he couldn't answer. What would *you* do, Mary?"

Before she could answer a green sedan swung off the tar road and braked in front of the gate. Two men climbed out, Mr. Sykes, who was driving, and Harlow Purdy. His father nodded in Roy's direction and followed Sykes to the gate. The foreman spoke briefly to the men on the other side. Roy couldn't hear; he did see him hand one of the guards a piece of paper, who turned and trotted down the road. He returned slowly with Kevin Olsen.

Kevin handed the paper to Sykes. "Open the gate at three when they come back," he told the men. Sykes and Harlow returned to the sedan. "Nobody comes in here but that car," Kevin ordered.

"The Association wants to talk to the strikers," Kevin told Roy and Mary. "They had a letter from the governor's office to let their man in. I had to agree. He has an offer to put to the men. The Association doesn't trust Barlow to deliver it, they said. I'll go tell the strike committee."

A little before three the green car returned. It came through the gate and down around the road to the grandstand. A man in a light suit emerged from the back. Sykes followed him, a megaphone in his hand. The man walked to the front of the grandstand which was almost full. He cleared his throat. "Can you hear me up there?" he began.

Some of the strikers high in the grandstand stood up. "No," they shouted. "Louder."

The man took the megaphone. He talked loudly. "What about now?"

171

"We can hear," a voice called down. "What do you have to say?"

"I am Richard Malone. I am head of the Growers' Association. The governor of the state has given me permission to come here and address you. I want to explain what the Association is prepared to do if you call off the strike. It's not doing either one of us any good. It's time for you and us to be reasonable."

"What's reasonable, mister?" an angry voice called from the crowd. "Starving our children ain't reasonable, I can tell you."

A murmur of agreement passed through the crowd.

"I'm as sorry as you are about what has happened," Richard Malone shouted. "I have told Mr. Sykes here that our Association will not tolerate any acts of violence. He has told me it was not his men who drove your food truck off the road."

Walt Landon stood up. "Then how come he was wearing a white shirt like your security men?"

It was Sykes who replied, "Lots of men wear white shirts."

"Please," Mr. Malone said, "let me tell you what we propose. Last week we made an offer in good faith of two cents a basket. Since then we have lost a considerable part of our crop. I wish I could tell you that offer still stands, but I cannot. We now offer a guaranteed one and a half cents a basket to the end of the season. In addition, we will open the campsites for a whole year— guaranteed. Last of all, we will deliver milk here and to the campsites in sufficient quantities for your children. That is all I have to say." Malone handed the megaphone to Sykes and got into the car. The pickers and

172

their families stared after it in stunned silence as it drove toward the gate.

"They'll take it," Barlow said to no one in particular.

"How do you know?" Roy asked.

"Because of the milk. They might starve themselves another week or so, but not their kids. They can see the thin faces and big eyes. The parents can't take that. Malone is a shrewd man. I'll meet with the committee, but it's all over."

As they came to the barn, horns blared from the gate. Two large trucks rolled past the cabins, the drivers shaking fists of friendship from open windows. Cheering strikers ran alongside. The trucks coasted down the grade to the cookhouse. The drivers jumped out and let the tailgates down.

"This will keep you going for a good while," one driver said. "They took up a collection, too. It's in here." He handed a canvas bank bag to Barlow. "Seven hundred dollars. Good luck, mate."

33

"The preacher is having a sunset service, Roy."

"Is it Sunday?" Roy asked. He was watching the road, hoping the yellow Stutz Bearcat would come racing back from Riverside. And he wondered about the green sedan that passed up and down in front of the gate regularly. It looked like the same car Sykes had driven the Association man to the grandstand in.

"Of course, it's Sunday, silly. Don't you know the days of the week?" Mary teased.

"I never paid much attention. I knew the days when I went to work and I had the Sundays when I went to see Dad marked on the calendar. When we headed west, I lost track. Here at the fairgrounds it doesn't make any difference what day it is. They all follow each other."

"And you know what else, Roy?" Mary whispered so the Kerr brothers, who were on guard duty at the gate, wouldn't know. "It's a secret, but I'll tell you. We're going to have a big picnic. Ma told me the women in the cookhouse are making potato salad and spareribs and

174

cake. With Kool Aid for the kids. What about that? Then the preacher is going to thank the Lord for looking after us and we'll sing songs like we did the first night of the strike. You'll take me to the picnic, won't you, Roy?"

"Sure," Roy answered. "See that green Oldsmobile going by, Mary? Isn't that Mr. Sykes's car?"

"I don't remember one car from another, unless it's that special yellow one you like so much. Ma is making chocolate cakes. The women took some of the money to the store with Mr. Gurney and bought everything they needed for the picnic. After tonight, it's back to the beans and rice, Ma said."

Roy stood up and ran to the gate. "Isn't that Sykes's car that just went by?" he asked Luther, who was on guard with his brother.

"I wasn't paying attention, Roy. What do you say, Reuben?"

"I don't know either. It was green, sure enough. It might have been."

"He's keeping track of us or something, I bet," Roy said. "Mr. Barlow warned they'd be up to something once they find out we can hold out a lot longer than they thought."

"I'd like to get back to work," Luther said, "even if it's picking oranges. Some men call this a vacation, but it don't feel right doing nothing all day long. I hope it's over soon."

Mary came over to the gate. "Walk me down to the cabin, Roy. Ma took my eighth-grade graduation dress from the trunk for me to wear to the picnic. It's time for me to change."

"Close your eyes, Roy," Martha Landon called from the doorway.

Roy turned his back and shut his eyes.

In a minute, another voice, Mary's this time, spoke. "You can turn around now."

Mary Landon stood in front of him wearing a white pleated dress with a wide red ribbon at the waist. Her hair was parted in the middle with a small red bow at each side. Roy could see a touch of powder on each cheek and smell the scent of perfume.

"What do you think, Roy?" Walt asked proudly. "She don't look like the same gal, does she?"

Roy held his breath. Mary was beautiful, more beautiful even than when he thought about her as he went to sleep. But something was wrong. "Where's your . . ." he began to say.

"I've been practicing without my crutches, Roy. Ma and Pa say it's such a special day I can try to make it to the picnic by myself if you'll help me along. Ma will bring them with her just in case."

Toby Wilder passed by. "You sure look sweet, Mary. Don't let her get away from you, Roy. Lots of boys at the picnic will be trying to steal her from you. I told Matty and the kids to walk along with you, Walt. I'll go relieve the Kerr boys. One man at the gate will do for an hour or two."

"Hold on, Toby," Walt said. "You stay with your children. I'll stand watch. Mother has Roy to go with Mary and her."

Toby protested, but Walt refused to listen. "It's a day for you to be with your family. You're all they have and it ain't right for you to leave them today." He strode toward the gate.

"It's true," Martha said. "It's a special day. All right, Mary, let's see you walk along. Take her arm, Roy."

The sun slipped behind the gathering clouds in the west. The preacher began to talk and, it seemed to Roy, talk and talk and talk. He sat with Mary and Martha halfway up the seats at the near end of the grandstand. He could hardly hear what the preacher was saying. It sounded like he was thanking the Lord for every good thing that had ever happened. Roy really wasn't listening. He held Mary's hand right in front of Mrs. Landon. He squeezed it every so often, and Mary squeezed back. He noted that the clouds were spreading toward Cordelia. They couldn't count the stars tonight. It might even rain.

Mr. Barlow had said they could win the strike. It was all over town that the Association had failed to get enough men from other places to save the crop for them. They would have to bargain with the strike committee. You could count on Mr. Barlow to see that the Association wouldn't let the growers put anything over on the striking men. Roy wondered if it was too late for him to be a lawyer if he went back to school. Dad wasn't going to stay with the goons if they lost the strike. He could live with Dad and maybe Mr. Landon could find a steady job nearby.

The preacher finished at last. The chorus gathered around him and began to sing. The people in the stands rose to their feet and joined in. It was completely dark now. Roy held Mary steady next to him and sang the words to the songs he knew. He sensed that the wind was picking up. It was going to rain. He sniffed. The wind brought a familiar smell. It wasn't the salt smell of the ocean, but it was familiar. He breathed in deeply through his nose.

Smoke! It was smoke, like the smell from the burning shack. Roy breathed in again. That's what it was. He looked over the crowd below toward the cabins and the buildings. There, in the darkness, he was certain he saw a flame shoot up from the barn.

It was fire. "Stay here," Roy ordered Mary. He pushed down to the bottom of the grandstand. To the men on the bottom planks, he said, "There's a fire at the barn." He raced around the end of the racetrack, men stumbling after him in the darkness.

Ahead of him the flames rose higher, whipped by the rising breeze. They illuminated the area around the barn and the cookhouse. Roy now saw the dark outlines of a heavy truck backed toward the buildings. A big man staggered from the Landons' cabin. It was burning inside. He threw a can into the truck and pulled himself up. Another man sprawled beside him.

With horror, Roy saw that the first man was Harlow. Next to him was George. "Dad!" he screamed. "Stop, stop!"

As the truck jumped forward, a group of strikers rushed in front of it. A rock crashed through the windshield. The truck careened off the road and smashed into a cabin. Immediately it was surrounded by angry men. They dragged Sykes from the cab and Harlow and George from the back.

Roy's father looked around him in confusion. He's drunk, Roy saw at once—like he was the night he set fire

178

to their shack, and Roy knew with certainty, like the night four and a half years before when Dad had taken the can of coal oil to the packing plant and burned it to the ground. Harlow was looking around the faces in the crowd for his son. Roy avoided his father's bewildered gaze.

Toby Wheeler ran back from the gate. He spoke to Kevin Olsen and Hank, then to Martha Landon and Mary who stood on the edge of the crowd.

Kevin pushed his way to Sykes. "The man at the gate is dead. You ran over him when you broke through."

"You're crazy," Sykes said. "The old fool wouldn't get out of the way. He was holding the gate shut. He stayed there holding on. I didn't kill him. He killed himself. He wouldn't get out of the way."

"It's murder," Peter Barlow said. He turned to Harlow and George. "Murder," he repeated. "That means you are murderers, too. God help you."

Martha was holding Mary close. The girl sobbed beyond control on her mother's shoulder. Dry-eyed, Martha reached out for Roy's hand. Tears now began to pour down her weathered cheeks. "Walt's gone, Roy, isn't he? He's gone, isn't that so?"

"He's gone, Mrs. Landon." He held Mrs. Landon's hand in his two hands like he would never let go. He understood that he had become a man. Men didn't cry. "But we're going to win, I bet. We can't lose now. We're going to win, all of us."

That wasn't enough. Nothing Roy could say would make much difference now, but Mrs. Landon and Mary had to have some words of comfort. "Remember what the preacher said just before we saw the fire? He said the good Lord looks after us in the time of our troubles and had sent us the food. He said when trouble came, we had to keep on going. He would help us along the way.

"You lost your husband and Mary lost her dad, and it looks like I lost my dad, too. There's no help for it now, so we just have to keep on going. Mr. Landon got us this far, looking after us. We have to keep on going without him, and someday we'll be all right again. I just know it's so. We'll be all right."